Brad had to be looking up her skirt.

Heat singed Elaine's cheeks. Her legs were apart and the skirt was hiked up to the tops of her thighs at this point. If he wasn't looking it would only be because he'd closed his eyes. Despite her best efforts to fo____ n pulling up into the cavernous area ____ ____ ceiling, she had to look down. Incre____ ____ re closed. She hauled hersel____ ____ ____ am and looked around. Lots ____ ____ ____ steel beams. She watched ____ ____ beam and pull himself u____ ____ climbing mountains his wh____ ____

"What now?" she a____ ____ ____ st slipped the tile back into its slot____ ____ grid system that supported the dropped c____ g.

"Should we—" Brad held up a hand, silencing her. Even in the near darkness she saw him tense. And then she heard it. Below, the bathroom door had opened....

DEBRA WEBB

A COLBY CHRISTMAS

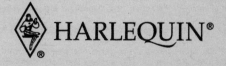

HARLEQUIN®

TORONTO • NEW YORK • LONDON
AMSTERDAM • PARIS • SYDNEY • HAMBURG
STOCKHOLM • ATHENS • TOKYO • MILAN • MADRID
PRAGUE • WARSAW • BUDAPEST • AUCKLAND

ISBN-13: 978-0-373-22951-2
ISBN-10:   0-373-22951-8

A COLBY CHRISTMAS

Copyright © 2006 by Debra Webb

www.eHarlequin.com

Printed in U.S.A.

ABOUT THE AUTHOR

Debra Webb was born in Scottsboro, Alabama, to parents who taught her that anything is possible if you want it badly enough. She began writing at age nine. Eventually she met and married the man of her dreams, and tried some other occupations, including selling vacuum cleaners and working in a factory, a day-care center, a hospital and a department store. When her husband joined the military, they moved to Berlin, Germany, and Debra became a secretary in the commanding general's office. By 1985 they were back in the States, and finally moved to Tennessee, to a small town where everyone knows everyone else. With the support of her husband and two beautiful daughters, Debra took up writing again, looking to mystery and movies for inspiration. In 1998 her dream of writing for Harlequin came true. You can write to Debra with your comments at P.O. Box 64, Huntland, Tennessee 37345 or visit her Web site at www.debrawebb.com to find out exciting news about her next book.

Books by Debra Webb

CAST OF CHARACTERS

Brad Gibson—He has been offered a position at the Colby Agency, but he may not be able to stay out of jail, or alive, long enough to accept.

Elaine Younger—The Colby Agency receptionist. It takes a near-death experience to propel Elaine into the land of the living. Can she trust Brad Gibson to help her stay that way?

Victoria Colby-Camp—The head of the Colby Agency.

Ian Michaels—Victoria's second in command and a man who knows how to spot trouble well in advance.

Lucas Camp—Victoria's husband. Will he make it home for Christmas?

Jim Colby—Victoria's son. He has a life-altering revelation for his mother.

Tasha Colby—Jim's wife. She is about to give birth to the first Colby grandchild.

Joseph Reynard—Building security.

Welton Investments—Brad Gibson's former employer.

Chapter One

December 23, 4:30 p.m.
Inside the Colby Agency

Christmas.

How could Christmas be here already? Day after tomorrow. The year had flown by.

Victoria Colby-Camp smiled as she watched the snow float down past the floor-to-ceiling window behind her desk. She loved the snow—loved this city. The flurry of pedestrians rushing to and fro on the street below made her tingle with excitement. Such vibrancy, such diversity, all rolled into one fabulous town.

Her smile stretched into a grin. And any day now she was going to be grandmother. A grandmother! Imagine it. For so many years her son had been lost to her. Just having him home again had been such a blessing. That he'd found a woman who loved him despite his horrific past was simply icing on the cake. But to be blessed with a grandchild, too, Victoria just didn't know how she could possibly be more fortunate. She had worried after last year's failed pregnancy. Thank heavens there had been no problems with this one. Her son deserved every moment of happiness that came his way.

The glittering lights draping every office and shop window twinkled especially bright this evening. Tomorrow was Christmas Eve and Victoria couldn't wait to share this special holiday with her family. She had very special presents wrapped and waiting to tuck beneath the tree for Lucas, Jim, Tasha and the coming grandchild. Watching their faces as they opened those gifts and anticipating their surprise had her giddy already and there were still twenty-four hours to go.

She glanced at her wristwatch, the tiny diamonds embellishing the face winking at her like the Christmas lights outside. Lucas had given her this watch for her birthday. She put it on every morning and cherished the feel of it against her skin. Her husband wouldn't be home until late this evening. She hoped there were no significant delays with inbound flights with this winter storm surrounding the city. She couldn't bear the idea of spending the holiday without him. The very idea sent an ache through her soul. That he'd had to rush off to Washington so close to the baby's arrival date had worried her, but Lucas had commitments to his work just as she did. She certainly couldn't deny him his work, even if she would prefer to have him all to herself every minute of every day.

Clearly she had grown quite selfish as she moved farther past the mid-century mark.

"Victoria, could I have a moment of your time?"

She turned around to face her personal assistant, Mildred Parker-Ballard, who waited just inside her office door. "Certainly, Mildred. Is everything on schedule for tomorrow?"

Mildred looked even lovelier than usual this morning. She wore her hair in a smartly coiffed pageboy style that flattered her oval face, and Victoria was certain she'd lost a few more pounds. Perhaps it was the recent workouts at the gym she and her new husband had joined. Or maybe it was nothing more than wedded bliss. Mildred and Dr. Austin Ballard had finally gotten married last month, in the very same church where a Ballard grandchild had been christened only weeks before.

Victoria had already ordered a very special christening gown for her first grandchild. She and Mildred had pored over magazines and catalogs for weeks before finding the ones they'd wanted in a local shop, where the gowns were handmade, one-of-a-kind creations.

Nothing was too good for the next Colby generation.

"Unless this storm takes a turn for the worst,"

Mildred assured, "all will go as planned for tomorrow's Christmas party."

Victoria clasped her hands in front of her. "Excellent." Anticipation welled in her chest. "Think, Mildred, how long it has been since we've had Trevor Sloan and Nick Foster here. I can't believe they were all willing to work their holiday schedules around the agency's Christmas party."

With her eyebrows arched high, Mildred peered at Victoria over her glasses. "Don't go jinxing things, Victoria. We still need the full cooperation of those big silver birds."

Mildred was right about that. Cancelled and delayed flights were par for the course around the holidays in Chicago. Thankfully most were traveling this evening or very early in the morning. Even Angel Parker-Danes and her enigmatic husband Cole were coming. Jack and Katherine Raine. And so many others. Victoria's pulse skipped with the mounting excitement. This would be the very best Christmas ever.

"You've touched base with the caterers one last time?"

Mildred nodded. "And the entertainment folks. In fact, they're coming in tonight after hours to set up their instruments and equipment in the big conference room. Elaine has kindly offered to stay and oversee their work."

Elaine Younger, the agency's receptionist. She

was very good at her job. Very pleasant, very dependable. But untouchable in so many other ways. Despite having been with the agency for more than two years already, she hadn't bonded with the rest of the staff as most new members did.

"I worry about that girl," Victoria said, voicing her thoughts to her closest confidant outside her husband.

"She's asked for tomorrow off again," Mildred commented, a note of concern in her tone as well. "She does it every year. It's as if she doesn't care for Christmas in the least. She never volunteers to help put up the decorations, but she's always more than happy to help take them down. I don't understand it."

Decorating the agency was a bit of an undertaking, Victoria wasn't so sure she could blame Elaine or anyone else for avoiding that task. Mildred required perfection. Still, it did seem odd that Elaine had no desire to join in any of the holiday traditions. The rest of the staff had welcomed her warmly when she'd come on board.

There appeared to be no rhyme or reason for her distance. And it certainly wasn't as if Elaine's parents lived far away, requiring that she leave the city early on Christmas Eve in order to be home for the holiday. She clearly didn't want to be a part of the agency's celebration and that saddened Victoria.

"I'll speak with her," Victoria offered. "Perhaps I can persuade her to drop by for a few minutes anyway."

Mildred lifted her shoulders in a noncommittal shrug. "I suppose it wouldn't hurt to try."

A rap on the door drew Victoria's, as well as Mildred's, attention there. Ian Michaels, Victoria's second in command, waited for an invitation to enter. He looked elegant as always in his black suit. Black shirt, black tie. The man always wore black. It was his trademark. Tall, dark and incredibly handsome as the saying went. There was just one difference in Ian's appearance today. He wore a little Rudolph pin on his lapel and the famous reindeer's nose flashed like a beacon. Victoria was entirely certain that one of Ian's children had insisted he wear it.

"Pardon me, ladies," he said in that charismatic voice that kept all the female employees swooning, and Victoria and Mildred were no exceptions. "May I have a moment of your time, Victoria?"

"I'll call Santa to make sure nothing's come up that would prevent him from appearing on time tomorrow," Mildred volunteered as she headed for the door. She smiled at Ian as she passed him. "If he's looking for Rudolph, I'll tell him to give you a call, Ian."

Victoria put her hand over her mouth to stifle a laugh at Ian's unamused expression. When Mildred had closed the door he strode straight up to Victoria's desk, his countenance turning infinitely serious as he neared.

"We may have a problem with Gibson."

"Please." Victoria gestured to a chair. "Sit. Fill

me in." The last she'd heard all was a go with the selection of the newest member of staff. Bradley Gibson had completed the series of interviews required, each done on his lunch break since he worked such long hours with Welton Investments down on the second floor of this very building.

Victoria and Ian had gone out of their way to facilitate the young man's schedule. Truth was, they wanted him that badly. Though he would be an investigator in training, Victoria had offered him a starting salary that he couldn't easily ignore. The agency needed a man with his caliber of expertise in the area of high finance. So many of their clients were snared into scams within that complex world it made perfect sense to employ the very best in the field to work on those cases. Hence Bradley Gibson had been wooed away from Welton. Victoria wasn't the least bit apologetic. The young man had admitted to being unhappy in his present position for some time. She would hate to lose him at this point.

"A friend from the local Bureau office called to warn me about an imminent announcement that could possibly affect us if the media discovers Gibson is connected to our agency. Apparently they've been watching him and are aware of his visits to our offices."

Victoria let the frown tugging at her brow have its way. "What sort of announcement?" She'd been extremely impressed with Bradley Gibson. She couldn't believe her instincts had failed her so completely. Only once in her entire career had she misjudged a new hire and even that one time had turned out for the better of all concerned. The idea that the FBI had been watching didn't faze her. It was the new millennium; with terrorism at epidemic proportions, vigilance was essential.

"Apparently the FBI has had Welton Investments under surveillance for months now. My source wasn't at liberty to disclose the suspected charges, but I can hazard a guess. Money laundering, perhaps embezzlement. In any event, it appears our Mr. Gibson may be one of the top players involved in this distasteful business. The warrants will be served late tomorrow afternoon, ironically at approximately the same time that our holiday party is scheduled. That's as much information as he could give me and I doubt I would have gotten that much had he not owed me a tremendous debt."

Victoria could see where he was going with this. "You think we should withdraw the invitation we made to Mr. Gibson that he join our holiday celebration? Let this play out without our involvement?"

Ian propped his elbows on the arms of the chair, steepled his fingers and considered his response a moment. "I believe we should do what's best for the agency. If the media gets wind of this sting, they'll be right behind the arresting agents. You know there's always a leak to the press. The Bureau likes every move they make to be high profile."

A former U.S. Marshal, Ian was married to a former FBI agent. But Victoria didn't need Ian or his lovely wife Nicole to spell out how this would go down. She'd been in this business long enough to know it wouldn't be pretty.

"Tell me, Ian." She sat back in her chair and studied the one man she felt with absolute certainty could run the Colby Agency every bit as well as she. She trusted his judgment implicitly. "It's not that I'm dismissing the Bureau's assessments, but did you get any sense whatsoever that Mr. Gibson was anything other than what he presented in our interviews?"

Ian moved his head from side to side. "This feels exactly like a setup. Of course, there is always the risk that I'm wrong, but I believe Mr. Gibson may need us far more than we need him just now."

"We can't exactly warn him," Victoria confessed, more for her own benefit than Ian's. As much as she'd like to help Mr. Gibson with his coming woes, the agency fiercely protected its many sources. Without those sources they could never accomplish the results Colby Agency clients had come to expect. However, she felt obligated on some level to the young man.

"No, we can't warn him." The glint in Ian's eyes told her he had a plan. "We can, however, bring him in early for one final test in an attempt to preempt tomorrow afternoon's untimely episode."

"You want to explore more deeply any problems he may be having with his current employer?" Ian couldn't outright ask about any suspected wrongdoing but he could pose theoretical questions that might prompt certain responses.

Ian nodded. "And I'd like to invite O'Brien to sit in."

Victoria nodded her understanding. "Outstanding idea." The newest Colby Agency investigator on staff, besides the two new recruits they'd hired a few months ago, Patrick O'Brien was a former college professor. Not just any sort of college professor, he'd achieved his Ph.D. in psychology, which technically made him Dr. Patrick O'Brien. But he preferred not to be addressed that way. His absolute brilliance when it came to the human mind was uncanny. Victoria wasn't sure Mr. Gibson would appreciate an on-the-sly analysis, but she wanted to give him the benefit of the doubt where the accusations against him were concerned. This route would be discreet and, hopefully, helpful to all involved.

"Shall I see if Mr. Gibson is available during his lunch hour tomorrow?" Many of the offices were either closed or shut down early on Christmas Eve. Like the Colby Agency, Welton Investments was not one of those.

Ian stood. "I'll make arrangements with O'Brien before I leave for the day."

Almost five o'clock. "Very good. I'll let you know if I can't reach Mr. Gibson."

Victoria entered the number as Ian left her office. When the receptionist two floors below completed her company spiel, Victoria said, "Brad Gibson, please."

The moment's hesitation that followed set Victoria on edge. Even before the woman's response finally came, dread had started to well all too rapidly. "I'm sorry, but Mr. Gibson..." She cleared her throat but even that didn't stop it from wobbling as she continued. "Mr. Gibson is no longer with this firm."

Victoria thanked the woman and placed the handset in its cradle. She immediately buzzed Ian, but he was already back at her door.

"Gibson is missing," he said as he moved into her office. "My source just called. Apparently Gibson didn't show up for work this morning. An hour ago a neighbor reported that his apartment door was standing open. The apartment was ransacked. No clues as to what was taken, at this point. No body was found but there was a considerable amount of blood. Forensics is attempting to determine if the blood belongs to Gibson."

Uneasiness added a few extra beats per minute to Victoria's heart rate. This didn't feel right. She'd spoken to this man on several occasions. Bradley Gibson was no bad guy and he certainly wasn't a killer.

"Let's put someone on this, Ian. The boys at the Bureau won't like it, but I can't let this go without seeing if there is any way we can help Mr. Gibson." Dead or alive, she didn't add.

"I'll look into the case myself," Ian offered.

"I would appreciate that. This doesn't feel right."

Victoria sat very still for a long moment after Ian had gone. It was almost Christmas….

She stood and moved back to her spacious window. The snow was falling harder now—big, lush flakes. Life was so fragile. All that one cherished could be lost in a mere instant.

She offered a quick, silent prayer for Bradley Gibson.

This would not be such a happy holiday for him.

Chapter Two

December 23, 7:45 p.m.

The sound of children laughing woke Elaine Younger from a dead sleep.

She sat straight up and pushed the hair out of her face.

The office…she was still at the office.

She could feel the imprint of her forearm marred into her forehead. She rubbed at it with the heel of her hand.

The sound she'd heard had come from the radio. Christmas music…"Santa Claus is Coming to Town."

Disgust groaned out of her as she pushed up from her desk. She'd listened to that stuff all day long, every day for the past three weeks. Enough already.

She moved around her desk and headed for the lounge. The media control center was in the lounge supply room. Everyone else had already gone home except her. She could turn off the music now and no one would care.

It was nearly eight. Where the heck were those musicians? Hadn't Mildred said they'd be here about seven? Just her luck that they'd be running late. She couldn't believe she'd fallen asleep at her desk.

Elaine flipped on the overhead light, crossed to the far side of the lounge and went into the supply room, where cases of soft drinks and other refreshments, as well as stacks of napkins and disposable cups, were stored. She opened the control panel door and entered the sequence to shut down the piped-in music.

The silence that followed was truly golden.

She nabbed herself a bag of chips and a bottle of water before turning off the lights and heading back to her desk. Maybe she'd call security and see if they'd heard anything. If the musicians weren't coming until tomorrow morning there was no reason for her to hang around.

Maybe there'd been a miscommunication but she doubted it. Mildred never got things like that wrong.

Elaine had the day off tomorrow. She couldn't wait to get home and plug in an action flick—anything to escape the holiday hoopla. Her folks would call at nine and they'd talk about whether to have hard rolls or soft with the ham. It wasn't as if

Christmas had ever been a big deal with her family. She didn't get why the whole world had to go into such major pandemonium over this time of year.

Christmas should be private…without all the fuss.

She'd just popped a chip into her mouth when her line rang. Hurrying to her desk, she washed the chip down with a sip of water. If she were lucky that would be security letting her know the musicians had arrived. She placed the bag of chips and bottle of water onto her desk and grabbed the phone.

"The Colby Agency."

"Yes, ma'am, this is Joseph in security. I'm at the front door and there are three gentlemen here who say they have to set up their instruments on your floor."

"Thank you, Joseph. This is Elaine Younger and I've been expecting them. Please send them up."

"They're going to have to use the freight elevator, Miss Younger. Some of these cases are quite large."

"That's fine, Joseph. Whatever works best. I'll meet them at the freight elevator."

"Yes, ma'am."

Elaine dropped the receiver back onto its cradle and hurried around behind her desk to get the ring of keys, including the one for the freight elevator. She scratched around in the middle desk drawer. Didn't see anything even remotely resembling keys. Where the heck had she put them? "There you are." She grabbed the bracelet-style key ring, automatically slid it onto her wrist, and headed to the west end of the building.

The freight elevator was set up to allow stops on any floor in the building, but only an authorized employee on each floor could enter the necessary approval code for the elevator doors to open. A key was required to access the digital control pad.

The Colby Agency encompassed the entire fourth floor. The main elevators stopped in the lobby, directly in front of Elaine's desk. From the lobby, a wide main corridor to the left of her desk led past the conference room, restrooms, the lounge and the offices of several of the highest ranking investigators. At the end of that main corridor was Victoria's suite of offices, including the one belonging to Mildred, as well as the emergency exit to the stairwell. That was where the main corridor ended, but a slightly narrower hall took a right from there and moved around the perimeter of the building, coming to an end at the freight elevator. Along that long, L-shaped hall were several additional smaller offices, the massive research department, the files room and a larger main supply room.

The agency's last remodeling had included extensive decorating changes, including new carpeting and lush furnishings, for every square foot. Even the files and supply rooms were aesthetically appealing.

Elaine didn't rush. It would take a few minutes for

the musicians to load up their goods and set the elevator in motion. Joseph had said that some of their cases were pretty large. She wondered about that. Wasn't the entertainment for tomorrow's party supposed to be a small three- or four-piece band?

Oh well. She knew nothing about the equipment required to put on a musical performance. For the first time she wondered how long it would take for these guys to set up. She'd be lucky to be out of here by ten.

Elaine rolled her eyes and picked through the keys on the ring to locate the right one. Well, it wasn't as if she had any real plans anyway. She pushed the designated key into the lock and turned it to the right. The door opened, revealing the keypad.

She got as far as the second digit of the code when the lights went out.

Total darkness swallowed her up for the space of two heartbeats before the emergency lights kicked on.

Elaine let out the breath she'd unconsciously held. "Well, okay, then." No electricity. No elevators.

She did an about-face and strode back in the direction of her office.

Blackouts in the dead of winter weren't unheard of but they were generally precipitated by a serious snow or ice storm or plummeting temperatures. It was still snowing outside, she noted as she walked briskly down that long semi-dark hall, but it wasn't that bad. She hesitated a moment or two to stare out that long wall of glass. Just a thick dusting on the ground so far. No big deal.

But there were lots of other things that could cause this kind of power outage. A major traffic incident involving a relay station would do the trick. The system could be overloaded. It was damned cold outside. She chafed her arms. Getting chillier in here as well. She should have grabbed her sweater.

When she reached Victoria's suite of offices and the wider corridor beyond, she had the almost over-whelming urge to break into a run.

Ridiculous. She'd been here alone at night dozens of times. This wasn't the first time the power had failed. Falling asleep at her desk had her feeling off balance. Not to mention she was running on overload herself where the holidays were concerned.

"Sheesh," she muttered, "that's it."

The holidays. The whole city was decorated to the max, especially with lights. Lots and lots of extra lights. No wonder the power had failed.

At her desk she snatched up the receiver and entered the number for security. She waited through ring after ring. No one answered. Joseph was probably at the freight elevator with the musicians and their equipment.

"Damn."

Usually there were two guards. Why didn't the other guy answer?

"Don't panic." Both guards were likely busy doing whatever had to be done during a power outage. She should just calm down.

She had two choices. She could either wait for the power to resume or she could hustle down to the main lobby and see what was going on. It would be just her luck that halfway down to the first floor the lights would kick back on and she'd have to run back up to authorize the freight elevator doors to open.

Waiting was the best course of action. If she were wrong, Joseph or the other security guard would call and let her know what she should do.

Not a problem.

While she waited she tidied her desk. Separated the few messages she'd taken the last couple hours of the workday. Each investigator had his or her own slot in a carousel on her desk. Victoria's messages were passed on to her assistant, Mildred. The week's supply requests lay in a neat stack in Elaine's inbox. She inventoried and ordered general office supplies each week. Any requests beyond the usual were dropped off in writing for her to have authorized. Mildred did the routine authorizing. Most of the time she helped Elaine check in the supplies when they arrived. It was a relatively big job, definitely made for two.

All in all Elaine liked her position here at the

Colby Agency. She stepped back and considered her work area in the meager light.

Most of the time she liked it. Things got stressful at Christmas. Investigators were working hard to wrap up their assignments. Holiday work schedules were a pain in the rear. Everyone wanted extra time off between Thanksgiving and New Year's. Elaine was glad she didn't get that same fever.

The holidays were, for the most part, just another day to her.

Last year she'd taken up Mildred's slack so she could be off for her niece's wedding preparations.

That was another big deal here at the Colby Agency. Weddings. Oh, yes, and births. The entire staff operated more like a large family than a group of unrelated employees. At times she found the pressure to be involved tedious.

Regardless, the Colby Agency was the best. She had to admit that. No matter how high-profile and complex, or how small and seemingly insignificant the assignment, the job always got done. That was the major reason she stayed. She could put up with most anything to be on the winning team.

Ten minutes passed.

Still no call. Still no power.

The memory of opening that control panel door and starting to enter the code for the elevator pushed to the forefront of her thoughts. She'd turned around and walked back to her office. She'd noticed the snow still falling outside. The dusting on the ground below.

And the lights.

She whirled toward the wall of windows behind her desk.

The whole city was lit up like a giant Christmas tree.

If there was a blackout, why wasn't anyone else affected?

Her full attention glued to the lights outside, she moved to the window and stared down at the street. There were still a few pedestrians on the sidewalks. Not a single building anywhere in sight was dark.

What the hell was going on?

She called security again.

This time she got a strange busy signal, the kind that more often meant something was wrong with the phone line.

Fine. She'd just have to go down to the main lobby and find out what the problem was. It might be silly of her, but she couldn't just wait around here. She reached under her desk to fish her cell phone from her purse. Her concern might be for nothing but she wasn't about to head down a dimly lit stairwell in a deserted building without her cell phone. Maybe she'd seen one too many horror flicks.

Phone in hand, she strode determinedly toward the end of the corridor, where the emergency exit provided handy access for the head of the agency.

She twisted the knob and pushed but the door didn't budge. Wait a minute. She stepped back and surveyed the door. This wasn't right. It was an emergency exit. Emergency exits weren't ever supposed to be locked.

Jiggling the knob again she had to admit defeat. It was definitely locked.

A spurt of mild panic surged in her chest.

Okay. Stay calm. There had to be an explanation for this. She looked at the ring of keys she'd shoved onto her wrist. She was the keeper of the keys. There had to be a key on here for this door as well, though she didn't actually recall having been told about one. More than two years had passed since her initial training. Maybe she'd forgotten.

Using trial and error, she tried one key after the other to see if one opened the door. Wouldn't you know it, the final key she attempted did the trick.

Thank God.

This was totally weird.

She stepped into the stairwell, let the door close behind her with a distinct click. Like most people she preferred the elevators so she'd only been in the stairwell once or twice. Both times for a fire drill.

Even with the emergency lights the gloom gave her the shivers. Layers of beige paint on the walls, railing and stairs didn't help. No windows. She shivered. Damned creepy at this time of night.

This whole power outage thing had spooked her unreasonably. She left the office after dark most of the winter. What was the problem here? She shook off the lingering feelings of foreboding. All she had to do was go downstairs and locate Joseph or the other guard. Service to the phone on the security desk may have been disrupted with the power outage.

Grasping the rail to steady herself, she moved down the stairs. No need to get in a hurry. Now would not be a good time to fall and break something. She might not be discovered until morning. Ian Michaels and several of the other investigators all took the stairs on a regular basis.

Third floor. She wondered vaguely as she passed if that door was locked as well. That part still puzzled her. What good was an emergency exit if it were locked?

Other than the tap of her boot heels, the stairwell was eerily quiet. But then it would be. Every single soul who worked on the premises other than she and the two security guards had likely gone home already.

She was never in that big of a hurry to leave work. It was just her and her tiny apartment. No one waited for her, not even a dog or cat. She'd thought about getting one but then she'd worry that if she had to stay late at the office the animal would be alone too much. Her evenings usually consisted of going home, heating up a frozen dinner in the microwave and then getting lost in a movie. Horror, action, comedies, she liked them all. Once in a while her neighbor invited her out to dinner, but they really didn't have that much in common.

And dating. Well that was a joke. The closest thing she'd had to a date recently was when the guy at the video store had asked her to hang around to have coffee with him on his break. That hadn't lasted beyond his fifteen-minute break.

Second floor. Still quiet as a tomb.

Not that she was feeling sorry for herself. She liked her life just as it was. No dramatics, no extra pressure. Just plenty of time to enjoy being who she was.

One of the new guys hired in last spring's job fair had flirted with her at first. Todd Thompson. But he'd ended up marrying his first assignment. Most of the other investigators considered her their little sister or something. They sure didn't look at her with an eye toward dating.

Definitely not.

It wasn't that she was hideous to look at or anything like that. She was thin, without really trying. She actually looked younger than her twenty-six years. She wouldn't likely be winning any beauty contests, but she had a nice face. Big brown eyes. That was the part about herself she liked best. Not that she dwelled on how she looked. She didn't. She didn't waste money on designer clothes, either. She shopped at the more reasonably priced discount stores, which ensured she had a healthy savings.

Maybe she'd take an exotic vacation one of these days.

Maui, Cancun, someplace warm with sandy beaches.

When she reached the door that would open into the wide corridor that led into the first-floor main lobby she found it locked as well.

This was too weird. First thing Monday morning she would call maintenance and have this situation looked into. If that didn't take care of the problem she would call the fire marshal. What if she hadn't had the keys and there had been a fire?

The building could go up in flames and she wouldn't be able to get out. Definitely against the rules. Someone would be in serious trouble.

She shuddered as she twisted the key in the lock. A person never thought of things like that until they were thrust into the situation.

Beige décor gave way to marbled floors and soaring ceilings as she followed the short corridor that spilled into the main lobby. The ambience was every bit as posh as one would expect in a building with such elite tenants.

The lighting wasn't much better down here. The higher ceilings and towering glass front entry provided some additional illumination from the city lights.

Her heels clicked on the marble as she crossed the massive space. Even down here it was graveyard silent.

Bizarre.

The security desk was unmanned.

No sign of the musicians for tomorrow's entertainment. Or their cases of equipment.

Maybe Joseph had escorted the gentlemen to the freight elevator already. But where was the other guard? And, considering they couldn't board the elevator, why hadn't Joseph returned? Then again, maybe the musicians were stuck on the elevator and Joseph was trying to help.

Still, leaving the security desk unmanned was completely unprofessional. Victoria would be extremely disappointed that security turned so lax after hours.

Admittedly Elaine had never stayed quite this late, but she'd never known security to just disappear.

Something had to be wrong.

Calling 911 might be overreacting but she wasn't about to pretend any longer that things were as they should be. She'd run out of excuses.

Elaine moved around to the back of the security desk. Her foot caught on the same object her gaze had landed on the instant she rounded the corner of the desk, only her brain hadn't accepted the analysis just yet.

Joseph.

A scream rushed into her throat but fear had clamped shut the muscles in her neck.

Her body trembling, she lowered into a crouch and touched him. A dark stain had spread out from a small hole in the center of his chest. The navy color of the uniform distorted the color but she knew it was blood.

He'd been shot.

A surge of air rushed into her lungs, forcing her heart to race. Some part of her screamed at her to cry out for help, but some other part, a deeply entrenched instinct she hadn't known existed until now, kept her silent.

Her fingers shaking, she touched his neck. No pulse. His skin was too cool. Was his heart still beating? No heartbeat.

She got into position for CPR, except she couldn't feel any breath on her cheek. No rise and fall of his chest.

Tilting his head back, she opened his mouth, ensured the airway was unobstructed and forced air into his mouth. Something was wrong. The lungs didn't expand…chest didn't rise. She tried again. Nothing.

Oh, God.

She moved into position over his chest and attempted compressions. She worked until her arms were so weak she couldn't press anymore.

He was dead.

She had to call for help. She should have done that first. But she'd panicked.

Her phone. Where was her cell?

She'd had it in her hand.

She must have dropped it when she found Joseph.

But where was it?

Pressing her cheek to the floor she peered under the security desk. There it was. She couldn't reach it, needed something to reach under there and drag it out.

Maybe the phones down here worked.

She scrambled to her feet, almost tripping over Joseph's body. Grabbing the phone, she pushed a button for an outside line but got no dial tone. She stabbed another one. Nothing.

Fear roared through her.

What the hell was wrong with the phone?

She poked buttons until she'd tried every line available. Still no dial tone.

Okay. Her cell. She'd just have to get her cell from under this desk. There was no way in hell she could move it. It was huge. She needed a ruler or something else long and flat to sweep the phone from under the desk.

Just then movement on the security monitors captured her attention.

Two men. She saw two men clad completely in black, including ski masks. As she watched one opened a large trunk. Another man, dressed the same way, rose up as if rising from a coffin and climbed out. A second trunk was opened to reveal another man.

Large cases.

The musicians?

Why would they have masked men hidden in their equipment cases?

And where the hell was the other security guard?

She peered at all four of the monitors stationed on the counter. Two were designed to change channels every few seconds, providing views of different floors and corridors. No movement anywhere but *there.* Where was that? Then she saw it…the freight elevator.

First floor.

Terror lit in her blood.

Two of the men exited the range of the camera but returned in seconds lugging…a body.

She identified the uniform. The other security guard.

Her breath trapped in her lungs.

The men dumped the body into one of the cases. Closed and locked it.

She stared at the monitor…her ability to think frozen with absolute fear.

Wait. Where were the other two men?

No sooner had the thought formed than the man still on camera, using a key ring similar to the one on her wrist, attempted to activate the freight elevator.

No power. No elevator.

She had to call the police.

Frantic now, she dug through the drawers. Couldn't find anything longer than an ink pen.

She glanced at the monitor. Two men waited by the freight elevator. Movement on another monitor. Two men…moving down a corridor. Marble floors.

They were coming back to the lobby.

She had to hide.

Stumbling over Joseph, she landed hard on the floor.

She scrambled to her feet. Realizing the boots would make too much noise, she frantically tugged them off.

She had to run.

Now.

There was no place to go except…she frantically searched her memory banks for any sort of hiding place.

The snack shop.

Closing her fingers around the keys that dangled from the ring on her wrist to keep them quiet, she rushed past the elevators, almost falling when her feet slipped. Damn these tights. Running as fast as she could without making any sound or busting her butt, she didn't let herself look back. Couldn't slow down for anything.

The shop was closed but half a dozen tables and chairs were scattered around its entrance. She crouched behind the table closest to the wall, hoping the chairs would provide sufficient camouflage. There were three other tables staggered in front of the one she'd chosen. Surely they would provide additional coverage…enough so no one would see her.

Thank God she'd worn her favorite dark brown skirt and turtleneck today, as it helped her to blend in with the dark metal legs of the table and chairs. If she were brutally honest with herself she'd probably only selected the drab colors as an act of rebellion against the reds and greens of the holiday fanatics.

Whatever the reason, she was damned glad she had. Except for the tights. Running in them was dangerous. She bit her lip. She should get rid of them now to ensure she wasn't sorry later. Careful not to make a sound she wiggled the damned things off her hips and down her legs and stuffed them into the closest chair. She shivered as the cool air replaced the warm woolly fabric against her skin. Freezing to death was preferable over being murdered.

The two masked men moved around the security desk. They hefted Joseph's body and started back in the direction they'd come. He'd be hidden in one of the cases just like the other guard.

Maybe once they were gone she could risk going back after her cell phone.

She held as still as possible. Listened as their footsteps faded. She hadn't heard them approaching until they were far too close for comfort, but then they hadn't been carrying a body.

Once the silence had lasted to the count of ten, she

grabbed her boots and hugged them to her chest as she cautiously slipped from her hiding place.

Holding her breath, she tiptoed as fast as she dared back to the security desk. Avoiding the blood splatters, she dropped down onto her hands and knees and tried to shove her hand under the desk.

She couldn't reach it.

She tried harder and felt the sting of blood where the wood skinned the top of her hand.

Dammit.

She worked until she'd threaded one of her boot legs under the desk, but it wouldn't reach.

Frustrated, she rose up. Jammed her fingers through her hair. There had to be something around here she could use to reach that damned phone.

A hand slapped down hard over her mouth as she was jerked backward.

She struggled to get away…but it was no use.

Chapter Three

"We have to get out of here. Now."

Elaine couldn't see the man's face, but he didn't sound as if his intention was to harm her. Still, the words whispered so harshly against her ear had her heart shuddering with terror. What was going on here?

"I'm going to turn you loose, Elaine, but you have to promise me you won't scream."

Elaine? Who was this guy? She twisted in an attempt to get a look at him. All she got was a glimpse of blond hair and maybe gray eyes before he tightened the arm he had banded around her, keeping her from any further movement.

"Promise?"

He was waiting for a guarantee from her before he let go. She nodded, prayed she'd be able to stick by her word. Who was this man?

"Okay. As soon as I've released you, we have to make a run for the stairwell. Understand?"

Why would he want to go back to the stairwell? She needed to get to her phone. Joseph…her stomach roiled. Poor Joseph was dead…so was the other guard. She wasn't sure about the second guard, but she knew Joseph had a family. A wife and three kids.

"Do you understand?"

She nodded at his sharply whispered demand.

"All right."

His arm loosened and his hand came away from her mouth. Before she could stop her automatic instincts she'd scrambled away from him. "Who are you?"

He held a finger to his lips before shifting his attention to the monitors on the counter. Her gaze darted there as well. Staying alive meant staying away from those men.

Joseph's body had already been locked in one of the cases lined up next to the freight elevator. But none of the masked men were in view of the cameras. Just those big equipment cases that now served as coffins.

Fear shivered over her skin leaving goose bumps in its wake. They could be anywhere…right around the corner.

"There they are."

Her attention focused on one of the monitors. Fourth floor. A new kind of tension whipped through her.

Two of the masked men were exiting the stairwell door into the Colby Agency.

"What're they doing?"

She hadn't realized she'd said the words aloud until the man next to her had changed his position so that he could look her in the eye.

"Looking for you."

A quake started deep down in her belly. He was right. The guard had called her and asked permission for them to come up. These men knew she was in the building…on the fourth floor.

The Colby Agency had many enemies. She'd always known, had been thoroughly briefed on the potential, that this kind of situation could, theoretically, arise. There was always the chance that as a Colby Agency employee one might be targeted for revenge or coercion.

Elaine just hadn't expected it to be her.

She didn't know anything about cases, had never worked an investigation. Sure, she had access to most everything in the offices….

Maybe that was it.

These guys had come here under the pretense of setting up their equipment in order to accomplish their mission and somehow something had gone wrong. Either Joseph or the other guard had gotten suspicious and now the ugly truth was out. Now they were inside the Colby Agency. But why? Were they looking for files? Or was their agenda to lay in wait until the office reopened tomorrow morning?

She pushed the questions and thoughts aside. Right now, at this moment, she was the only representative of the Colby Agency on the premises. There was no one else. Not Simon Ruhl or Ian Michaels or any of the other brilliant investigators.

Just her.

"We have to stop them."

Her unidentified companion made a sound deep in his throat. "How do you propose we do that?"

He was right. How the hell could they stop these guys? The men wearing the masks were armed, were professionals so far as she could determine. She and—she glanced at the man next to her—this guy couldn't hope to do this alone.

"Do you have a cell phone?" Hers was still under the massive desk.

He gave his head a quick shake. "Lost it."

Well that made two of them. "Mine's under there." She pointed to the bottom of the security desk where it hovered just an inch or so above the floor. Why the hell did she have to have such a thin phone? If it had been just a little thicker it wouldn't have fit under there. From the corner of her eye she saw the blood on the floor. She shuddered, this time the reaction shook her visibly.

Two men were dead.

Her new friend in this nightmare motioned for her to move. Maybe he could reach her phone. She crept back from the desk so that he could lie flat down on the floor.

"We need something to sweep it out."

Duh. "I know, but I couldn't find anything, and then I got interrupted."

He scrambled back up to a kneeling position and reached for his belt buckle.

Her tension blasted to a new level. "What're you doing?"

"Maybe I can sweep it out with this." He wrenched the belt free of his trousers and flattened on the floor once more.

Elaine wrung her hands as she watched him thread the belt beneath the desk. If this worked they could have help on the way within minutes. Movement on the monitor hauled her attention upward.

Two of the masked men, weapons drawn, walked along a corridor.

Marble floor...

Damn. "They're coming."

The stranger still angling for her phone looked up at her. "What?"

"Two of those men are coming."

Somehow he was on his feet and dragging her away from the security desk by the time she said the last word. Her mind was still attempting to analyze the way he'd gone from on the floor to on his feet like an Olympic gymnast.

Time didn't permit them to make it all the way to the snack shop to hide. They were forced to crouch next to the row of self-service newspaper stands halfway between the security desk and the snack shop. For Elaine, curling into a ball was quite sufficient for staying out of sight. But the guy with her, his shoulders were too broad if he sat sideways and his legs too long to fold up compactly if he turned the other way. He had no choice but to flatten out against the wall next to her. If a sudden move were required he might be in serious trouble. Then again, he did appear able to move with amazing agility.

Elaine could hear the two men at the security desk. They rummaged through the drawers and doors beneath the counter, rifling things around, slamming drawers and doors. What were they looking for? Map of the building? Keys? The security guards carried a ring of keys on their belts. Most likely these criminals already had those. What else could they be trying to find? And why were the other two at the Colby Agency offices?

Holding her breath, she raised her head just far enough to peek over the tops of the newspaper stands. The two appeared to have given up on finding whatever they were looking for. One bent down, then straightened, the discarded belt in his hand.

Elaine's breath locked in her lungs. They'd never believe the belt had been left behind by one of the guards. She wasn't that lucky.

Familiar musical notes shattered the silence.

Elaine froze.

She knew that tune.

Her cell phone.

Damn.

It had to be nine o'clock. Her mother called her every night at nine.

One of the masked men got down on the floor and peered beneath the desk. Damn. Damn. Damn. They would know she'd been down here.

Using the same technique her still unidentified companion had started, the masked man fished out her cell phone. He waited until the music died and then he opened it. She could imagine him scrolling through her address book, checking her voice mail.

He closed her phone, dropped it on the floor and smashed it with the heel of his boot. She jerked at the violence behind the move.

The man looked up abruptly and surveyed the lobby, as if she'd telegraphed her displeasure straight to him.

Elaine ducked her head down.

She felt the man behind her stir. Clearly he'd recognized that it was her phone that had announced its presence.

If those two bad guys started in this direction…

Dread churned in her belly. There was no place to hide. If they even moved they could be spotted.

Even breathing might not be a good idea so she held her breath.

The soft rasp of a rubber sole against marble vibrated across her senses.

One of the men was coming.

Fear hurdled into her chest. Her heart reacted by skipping a beat.

What could she do?

The crackle of a radio broke the tension.

A quietly muttered yes sent a new wave of terror through her. Whoever answered his radio couldn't be more than half a dozen yards away.

More talk, too low to comprehend and fading. The man speaking was moving away.

She had to look. Just to be sure.

Blood roaring in her ears, she dared another peek above the top of the newspaper stands.

Both masked men were back at the desk, still looking for something. And then, as if God had answered her silent prayers at that precise moment, the two walked hurriedly away from the security desk. She tried to see where they went but she couldn't be sure if they returned to the stairwell entry or turned in the other direction that led to the freight elevator.

As if he'd been watching the whole thing through

her eyes, the man behind her was up and tugging her after him. How the hell did he do that?

She wanted to ask where they were going and what he planned to do but she didn't have the nerve to risk even a word. She couldn't be positive about how far the two killers had moved away from the lobby.

When he dragged her into the corridor—the same corridor which those two killers had taken— she balked.

"What're you doing?" Was he trying to get them caught? No, not caught—*killed.*

Again he held one finger to his lips and ushered her forward.

She stared with longing at the front entry. It would be so easy to make a run for it…but those doors would be locked and any attempt to get them open would trigger an alarm. Breaking the glass would take throwing a large chair or sofa through it, she imagined. But then, the bad guys would know their location and they would come. The cops would come, too, but the roads were slippery with the snow.

He'd pushed into the ladies' room before she'd totally given up on the idea of making a run for the nearest exit, alarm or no alarm.

He pressed his finger to her lips when she would have spoken. She couldn't read his intent.

She leaned against the closed door and hauled in a ragged breath. They were on the first floor. A towering wall of glass made up the front wall of the lobby. Could she draw someone's attention if she jumped around and waved out there? Would setting off the alarm be the right thing to do? Would the police arrive in time to save her before the bad guys got down to the lobby?

Probably not.

Focus, Elaine. She couldn't go off on a tangent. She had to keep her mind on the moment…on the man currently occupying the ladies' room with her.

He checked each stall to make sure they were alone. Then he walked with muted steps back to where she waited.

"Let's move away from the door," he suggested so quietly she barely heard him.

The urge to scream was almost overwhelming. People were dying and they were tiptoeing around and whispering.

She did as he said without argument, since she had no desire to give away their location. But now that they had some time to catch their breath she had a question or two for her anonymous ally.

"Who are you?"

She was pretty sure she had asked that before but there hadn't been time for an answer.

"My name is Brad Gibson."

A frown furrowed deep into her forehead, causing the ache she hadn't noticed until now to take hold.

Perfect. Everyone should have a headache when running from killers. She settled her attention back on the man standing between her and the long line of sinks on the wall. Brad Gibson. That name sounded vaguely familiar. She hoped like hell it wasn't because she'd heard it on the news.

"I'm sorry, Mr. Gibson, but that doesn't tell me a thing. Why are you in this building? Do you work here?"

She didn't recall seeing him, but then again, she was usually the first to arrive and the last to leave on her floor. Well, besides Victoria.

It was doubtful that she wouldn't remember seeing this guy though. He was, she realized upon closer inspection, really cute. Tall. Blond hair that looked just right for a shampoo commercial and steady gray eyes. Nice face. The tan-and-navy striped shirt paired nicely with his khaki trousers. The brown leather loafers kept his movements noiseless. She glanced down at the boots in her hand. Great-looking and warm but worthless when it came to stealth.

"Yes. I work—did work," he amended, "on the second floor at Welton Investments."

Did work. "Were you fired?"

"In a manner of speaking I suppose I was fired."

"Wait." She set her boots on the closest surface, the diaper-changing table provided for the convenience of the building's clients. She didn't know why she'd bothered hanging on to them after she'd shed her tights. Maybe because they cost half a paycheck and she wasn't generally the type to splurge. But in a city like Chicago, good boots were a firm investment. "You were fired and you're still in the building after hours?" Her gaze narrowed. Maybe this whole thing was about him somehow. But then why would those men have made the bogus appointment to set up equipment in the Colby Agency? Why would they be on the fourth floor at that very minute? And why the hell would they have killed two guards?

"It's not as bad as it sounds," he assured her.

She wasn't so sure about that but she'd give him the benefit of the doubt since he didn't appear inclined to harm her in any way. If she were totally honest he'd probably saved her life once already.

"Meaning," she prompted.

"It's a long story, Miss Younger. I'm sure you'd find it boring." He shoved that thick hair back from his forehead and massaged his temples with his thumb and middle finger as if he had a headache of his own. "Our priority right now needs to be about getting out of here alive."

Alive. She swallowed back a lump of uncertainty. He was right. These guys weren't kidding around.

"Why is the power off in this building? The rest of the city seems to be fine."

"Our visitors did that." He tugged at his collar as

if he were accustomed to adjusting a tie. "I guess they weren't expecting the back-up safety defense system."

"What back-up…whatever you said?"

"When they shut off the power, every internal door in the building equipped with a lock went into lockdown mode. Computers, phones, nothing can be accessed. The exit doors become unbreachable from the standpoint of attempting to pick the lock. It would take a small bulldozer to get one of those doors open now. There's no way anyone's leaving this building without a major effort and without tripping the alarm."

"Maybe we should trip the alarm."

"There's only two ways to do that." His gaze leveled with hers. "Break the glass in an outer wall."

"Or?" Did he have to look so resigned to their fate?

"Start a fire."

Damn, and she didn't even smoke. "You carry a lighter?"

That blond head moved from side to side. "You?"

A frustrated breath puffed past her lips. "Nope."

There had to be something they could do. Staying in this bathroom wasn't exactly a prime safe zone. It would only be a matter of time before the bad guys searched every damned room in the building looking for her. They might not know about Mr. Gibson, but they knew she was here. Those bastards might not be able to leave the building, but they had keys to every single interior door.

Then again, she thought as she glanced down at her right wrist, so did she.

"We can't stay in here." As safe as it felt right now, she knew that wouldn't last.

"We have to find a place to hide until—"

That he abruptly stopped sent a chill clattering along her spine. "What?" Had he heard something she didn't?

He set his hands on his hips and looked around the spacious restroom. "We should hide until it's safe to come out again. Just hide and stay hidden."

He'd just lied to her. Maybe not lied, but omitted something important. She might not be a trained investigator but she couldn't have missed that one if she'd tried. He hadn't even been able to look her in the eye as he'd made his statements. Statements she was pretty sure weren't what he'd started out to say.

"Right," she agreed. "We should hide out for sure." And here she'd thought she had herself a true ally in this war. She'd have to keep an eye on dear old Brad Gibson. He might look like the all-American boy next door, but she didn't trust anyone who would lie to her.

"Any suggestions?"

His gaze met hers this time. That he could go from lying to wholly sincere amped up her trepidation. Maybe he had some reason for avoiding the truth on a matter that didn't really have anything to do with the situation they were in.

And maybe Santa would be dropping by her house tomorrow night.

She couldn't worry about Brad Gibson's dependability just now. They had to hide. Someplace these guys wouldn't think to look in a million years. All she needed was a couple of years herself to figure out where that would be.

Inspiration nudged at her. She looked up. Those big rectangular acoustical tiles that indicated the ceiling was dropped somewhat below where it could be. She thought about how high the ceiling was in the lobby, then considered this one. There had to be large space up there above those tiles. There always was in the movies.

She pointed up. "How about up there?"

He considered her suggestion for a long moment, the muscles of his neck flexing as he studied the ceiling. She wondered if he'd been born with that healthy color or if he'd bought it at a local tanning spa.

"You could be on to something."

She blinked. Scolded herself for thinking about the tanned skin stretched over those toned muscles. To say this wasn't the time might be a cliché, but this definitely wasn't the time.

"Let's have a look up there." He angled his head toward the stalls and moved in that direction.

She followed him to the very last one. Since it was handicapped accessible there was plenty of room for both of them to be in the stall at once. And the toilet had a higher profile, which would facilitate what came next.

As she watched, Gibson closed the lid and climbed up onto the toilet. He reached overhead and pushed the nearest tile up and out of its designated slot. Climbing up through the opening he'd made would be the challenge. She estimated that Gibson was six or six-one. The ceiling was about nine feet off the floor, higher than the eight feet in her apartment but not quite as high as the ten in her parents' living room back home. The handicap accessible toilet sat up about two feet. Reaching the tile hadn't been a problem. All she could say was she hoped he had some good upper body strength to pull himself up there.

Gibson braced one foot on the large pipe at the back of the toilet that provided the handle for flushing. Pushing off from that foot, he reached for the open space and grabbed hold of something she couldn't see from where she stood. He just kind of hung there with that one foot braced on the plumbing for a second then he raised everything above his shoulders through the opening. She would bet he'd won the medal in the presidential fitness competition every year in school for chin-ups. She'd always stunk at those.

He eased back down onto the closed lid before stepping down to rejoin her on the floor.

"Steel beams," he explained. "They're fairly wide,

eight inches maybe. We can use those for a path. There's a whole maze of them up there." He thought for a moment. "We can follow the beams to any of the rooms on this level, including the elevator shafts."

"So we can hide up there?" The idea that hiding from those evil men might be that simple sent relief plummeting through her.

He nodded. "I think so."

"Can we stand up or is this going to be a crawling thing?" That thought deflated her hopes somewhat.

He visually measured her height. "You might manage it. I'll have to hunker over."

Didn't sound comfortable for him. But hey, this was every man for himself. To a degree anyway.

"So, are you game?"

If he meant was she going to do it, damn straight. "Let's do it."

He gestured to the toilet. "I'll give you a boost."

It wasn't until she stepped up onto the closed toilet lid that she considered another aspect of the situation.

She fixed Gibson with a warning glare. "If you look up my skirt, I'll kick you in the face." Boots or no boots that wouldn't be pleasant.

His only external reaction to her hostile warning was to blink. "I won't look up your skirt."

She tugged at her skirt, wanted it down as far as it would go. "See that you don't."

He climbed up next to her. The toilet lid creaked

under the added weight. The feel of his body positioned so close behind hers added another layer of tension to the moment.

She closed her eyes and steadied herself. She just wanted to get out of this alive. Him, too, she added.

"I'm going to lift you up," he murmured close to her hair. "Don't try to fight me. Just reach for the beam and pull yourself up. I'll give you plenty of help from down here."

Elaine took a breath. "Okay. I'm ready."

But she wasn't.

His hands closed around her waist and he lifted her as if she weighed nothing at all. Amazing. This guy had to do some serious working out.

"Grab onto the beam anytime."

The strained sound of his voice snapped her back to attention.

"Oh, sorry."

She spotted the beam and grabbed hold. Never an athlete, her upper body strength was pathetic, but she pulled with all her might. He had her by the feet now and was providing resistance for her to launch off of.

He had to be looking up her skirt.

Heat singed her cheeks.

Her legs were apart…the skirt was hiked up to the tops of her thighs at this point. If he weren't looking it would only be because his eyes were closed.

Despite her best efforts to focus on pulling up into the cavernous area above the ceiling, she had to look down.

Incredibly, his eyes were closed.

Impressed, she towed herself up onto the beam, straddling it as though it were a long skinny horse.

She looked around. Lots of wires. Acres of steel beams. And too damned many shadowy areas for comfort. Could be worse, since there were places where it was completely dark and the few emergency lights couldn't cover the entire space.

"Move it!"

She almost jumped at the harshly uttered command. "Gimme a minute." She had to get her bearings.

To avoid scraping her thighs along the beam, she got up on all fours and moved carefully away from the opening. She could probably stand up but she just wasn't ready for that yet.

He grabbed hold of the beam and pulled himself up and onto it as if he'd been climbing mountains his entire life and this was nothing.

"What now?" Was she supposed to sit there or did he want her to move farther along the beam?

"Let me get this back into place." He slipped the rectangular tile back into its slot on the grid system that supported the dropped ceiling.

The whole thing looked damned shaky to her. Not like these steel beams.

"Should we—"

He held up a hand, silencing her.

Even in the near darkness she saw him tense.

And then she heard it.

Below, the bathroom door whooshed shut.

Chapter Four

Brad Gibson couldn't see a damned thing below in the ladies' room, but he'd heard someone come inside. No mistake about that.

He'd like nothing better than to move, but any sound they made right now could give away their position and then this game would be over.

Game.

Right.

This wasn't a game. This was murder pure and simple. They wanted him dead and he didn't want to die.

He had plans.

His gaze strayed to the woman, Elaine Younger.

Enough innocent people had already died. Maybe his plan wasn't worth the cost. He could give himself up…but then no one would ever know the truth.

He wondered briefly if he should tell her the whole story, but that might be a mistake so he chose not to go there.

Not just yet anyway.

The sound of water splashing into a toilet bowl drew his full attention back to the room below. Evidently whoever was down there felt confident enough that no one was in the vicinity to relieve himself. A man didn't put himself in that vulnerable position unless he either had to go really badly or wasn't worried about being caught with his guard down.

Hard as he tried not to look at the woman caught up in this deadly chase with him, his gaze bumped into hers. She looked away faster than he did. They'd only just met and despite the fact that they were running for their lives the moment was awkward.

The sound of the door swooshing shut signaled that their company had made an exit.

Moving now would be a good thing.

Brad stood as best he could. He held onto the steel beam overhead that supported the next floor to keep himself steady. "Do you want me to lead?"

She glanced up at him without attempting to get to her feet. "If you have someplace in mind that would be good." She looked around. "I wouldn't have any idea where to start, much less where to end up."

He liked honesty. It was refreshing to find it in someone so easy on the eyes.

Elaine Younger was the Colby Agency's receptionist. Though he'd never seen her there during his visits, since she was usually at lunch, he'd watched her come and go late at night for about two years now. One of the security guards had told him who she was.

He'd thought he was the only person who stayed so late after work every night but she did as well. Case in point, here she was the night before Christmas Eve working late, as usual.

He held out his hand. She stared at it for a beat or two before deciding to grab hold. Pulling her to her feet would have been easy had she not been so nervous. She smoothed her skirt down and tried to look unaffected by their current dilemma but she wasn't anywhere near successful. She was afraid. That wasn't difficult to see. He didn't blame her. If he were honest, he'd have to say he was just a little afraid himself. For different reasons, maybe, but he felt fear all the same.

Her hair was a deep coffee-brown and fell around her shoulders in silky waves. Made her look very young. He wondered just how old she was. Big brown eyes. Big enough to give her a wide-eyed innocent appearance and that took him aback a little. Made him feel guilty for having some of the feelings he was currently having.

It appeared that even with death dogging him he could feel attraction.

Funny, he'd never considered himself the type for that kind of lusting. Fact was his social life was laughable. Maybe it was the extreme situation. Wasn't the fear of imminent death supposed to prompt the urge to mate?

"Hang on right here." He lifted her hand to the beam overhead. "I'll move around you so I can lead the way."

She looked uncertain. "Exactly how are you going to move around me?"

He touched his finger to his lips to remind her to speak softly. "Just hold on and you'll see."

While she hung on as instructed, he reached around her, got a firm grip on the beam just beyond her and then moved first one leg past her position and then the other. In theory it had seemed like a perfectly simple move, but in execution their bodies had been plastered together for about five seconds and that, considering his wayward thoughts, hadn't been a good idea. That she made this little sound, not quite a gasp but on that order, didn't help.

He took some time to consider their options, which were sorely limited. He wasn't so sure that moving upward would be to their benefit just yet. There wasn't any way to get out of the building from here unless they attempted to snake their way through a vent pipe of some sort.

The best course of action, in his opinion, was to

simply hide until the danger had passed. If those men couldn't find them surely they would leave.

Though the men appeared to be interested in the fourth floor, he was relatively certain this had to do with him and his former employer, Welton Investments, on the second floor. But then, he couldn't be absolutely certain. That he'd gone into his apartment that morning and found an intruder who tried to kill him lent a good deal of credence to his concerns that these masked men were here for him. The intruder at his place had been masked as well.

Brad took his time navigating through the labyrinth of wires and ductwork. He wasn't exactly sure what he thought he might find in the way of a place to hide, but maybe he'd know it when he saw it.

A place that looked safe to lay low for a while.

They'd covered most of the front side of the building when he found what he was looking for. A platform for working on what appeared to be part of the electrical system. Maybe a relay station or control panel for some part of the computer network. He wasn't an electrician or technician so he couldn't be sure. But the area would provide solid ground for hiding out. A railing on two sides would provide some amount of camouflage.

"Is this okay with you?" Might as well get her opinion before going any farther.

She surveyed the space. "Looks fine."

There wasn't much else out there. He surveyed

the massive space once more. This would have to do. He needed some time to think. Developing a plan would be a good idea but he didn't want to make any rash moves.

When they'd both gotten seated he leaned back against the railing that provided a safety barrier for anyone who might be working on the platform. He hadn't slept last night. Exhaustion clawed at him now. He kept seeing that man lying on his apartment floor, blood oozing from the wound in his chest. Brad hadn't meant to kill him. He'd never even had his hand on the gun, not really. They'd struggled and the weapon had discharged, a single hissing puff of sound. Brad had thought he was dead at first, but when the shock of realizing the weapon had fired had passed, it was the other man who'd lain still.

Before he could stop them, more of those images flashed one after the other. The tumble to the floor and the rolling around for control of the weapon had happened so fast. He shuddered inwardly, remembering the sharp jerk of the other man's hand when the weapon had fired. Brad had scrambled off the dead man and then he'd run. He'd heard a second man right behind him as he'd exited the rear of his building. It was a miracle he'd lost him in the crazy, zigzagging route he'd taken through that part of the city.

The second guy had shot at him only once. Thankfully he'd missed.

Sheer luck on Brad's part.

He knew nothing of running from bad guys, either. But he was damn sure learning in a hurry.

"So what happened with your job?"

The question snapped his eyes open. He hadn't meant to let his mind wander like that. His job. They were back to that again.

"Let's just say my colleagues and I had a difference of opinion."

"Then why did you stay after hours?" she asked, not cutting him the slightest slack. She wanted to know how he'd ended up in the building this late. She was suspicious already. "After all, tomorrow's Christmas Eve. Most people would give their eyeteeth for the day off. Don't you have someplace you would like to be?"

At least she didn't beat around the bush. "There's no place I have to be."

That might be a lie. He might have to be in jail or in the morgue, depending upon what happened tonight.

"You don't have any family?"

"Do you?" He turned his head to look her in the eye. Two could play this game of twenty questions. Those large, oval eyes made him feel guilty all over again for lying by omission.

"My parents live in Winnetka."

"Why aren't you on your way home?" Maybe if he drilled her she would back off.

She tugged at the hem of her skirt in an effort to

have it cover more of her thighs. Didn't work too well, which didn't bother him at all. She had very shapely legs. He wished he'd seen her when she was still wearing the boots, but he'd missed out on that.

"We do our holiday thing day after tomorrow." She picked at her blouse to keep from having to meet his eyes.

Holiday thing. Didn't sound like Miss Younger was to hip on Christmas. Now who was omitting?

"You have siblings?" May as well get the whole story while he was at it.

"Nope. Just me."

Ah. So they had something in common. "No siblings here, either."

"So, are you going home for the holidays?" She hadn't forgotten that he'd failed to answer her initial question.

"I usually do." He wasn't so sure this time. Jail or the morgue appeared far more likely. "I suppose if we get out of here, I'll go home." *If the authorities will let me,* he didn't add.

"You think we might not get out of here?"

The way those dark eyes peered up at him he was pretty sure he'd made a mistake with that comment.

He could tell her what she wanted to hear. That everything would be fine. That God wouldn't let them get killed this close to Christmas, but he wasn't so sure about that.

A lot could happen between now and dawn.

"We'll get out of here," he assured her, hoping she wouldn't pick on the underlying uncertainty. "Just not fast enough to suit me."

That appeared to placate her to some degree for about two seconds.

"I have another question."

He waited, hoping it wouldn't be anything else about his job. Or lack thereof, a voice reminded. Even if he got out of this alive and without going to jail, he felt reasonably sure the Colby Agency wouldn't want him now. That she didn't know about his offer at the agency made things a lot simpler. He didn't want to have to explain any of this to her. Hell, he really didn't even understand it himself. How was he supposed to explain it to anyone else?

"You said that the security system had some sort of backup safety measure. Why didn't it send a silent alarm to the police that we needed help?"

He didn't know the answer to that one. He was surprised himself about that. There should have been a backup in place for this very scenario. The police should be here already. But no one was coming. Those men had seen to that. He could only imagine that they'd overridden that part of the process somehow.

"Good question. I say we complain to someone about that on Monday."

If they were still alive on Monday.

Okay, enough with that. He was tormenting himself. But then he'd had that kind of day.

His future career was lost to him now.

His future, period, had gone down the tubes.

Was Elaine's part in this simply being in the wrong place at the wrong time? He didn't think so. He'd heard the guard named Joseph call her office about the supposed musicians who'd arrived. She had apparently been waiting for their arrival. He could only assume that they were part of the lavish Colby Agency party planned for the next day. The one he'd been invited to but wouldn't get to attend.

The unidentified men wearing the masks and wielding the guns had gained access to the building using that ruse. Their move had preempted his own. So, the question that begged to be considered was rather elementary, was this about him or the Colby Agency?

Or both?

9:58 p.m.

THIS NIGHT would never be over.

Funny, this was the first time he'd been with a beautiful woman in he couldn't remember how long and he couldn't wait for the night to end.

She was gorgeous and dedicated.

"Why do you stay late so often?"

He hadn't intended for that question to slip out but

there it was, on the table. He stayed late most every night, otherwise he wouldn't know she was staying late all the time. But asking the question would only lead to more questions about him from her.

"Someone has to do it."

The stock answer of all workaholics.

He'd used that one on numerous occasions himself.

"Besides," she went on, "I get a lot more done when everyone else is gone. I like the quiet."

This was truly scary. Her every answer echoed the ones he'd used for as long as he'd been in the work-force. She was far too pretty to be a slave to her work. That should be saved for guys like him who didn't have a social life.

"You…" She sat up straighter, her gaze narrowed. The one word reeked of accusation as if she'd just remembered that he'd cheated her or stolen from her before.

"You stay late all the time. That's where I remember your name from. I was leaving late one night and I got a glimpse of you striding across the parking lot. I wasn't sure I wanted to leave with you out there but the guard said you worked in the building as well. He said you worked late every night. Apparently that was on one of the rare nights that you left before I did."

Well at least he didn't have to worry whether or

not his new friend wondered if he were telling the truth about his former employment.

Up until a couple of days ago anyway.

Apparently the guards did a lot more talking than he'd suspected. One had told him about the backup security system otherwise he wouldn't have had a clue what happened tonight. Who knew? Maybe the guards just got bored.

"What went wrong with your job?"

There she went again. "Do you always interrogate people or is tonight just special?"

"Sorry. I was just trying to pass the time." She shifted and stretched her back, sending the skirt farther up her thighs. "Do you think they're still down there?"

"Probably."

He concentrated on visually scanning the area. He didn't want anyone sneaking up on them. Getting distracted with watching her every move wouldn't be good, either.

Several minutes passed with neither of them speaking. The reprieve allowed him to relax. It wasn't that he minded talking to her—he didn't. But he couldn't answer some of the questions she asked. Not without putting a wedge between them. If she thought he were some kind of criminal, she might refuse to work with him. Right now, he needed her cooperation. Saving both their lives might very well depend upon their being able to work together.

"I've been thinking."

He suppressed a groan. He should have known the silence wouldn't last.

"I'm not sure staying put here is the right thing to do."

That she would suggest putting herself back in the line of fire surprised him. "Going back out into the open could have less than pleasant repercussions and we need to consider what we would hope to accomplish." At least he needed to do that. He had a mission, one he couldn't put off for much longer. Granted, there was a new glitch. Keeping *her* safe.

"True, but if those men are trying to steal files or information from my agency, I should be attempting to stop them."

He turned his head in her direction and stared down his shoulder at her. "Are you serious?" That her loyalty would extend so far shocked him a little. A receptionist who was ready to defend the ship, so to speak?

Shocking and utterly appealing.

"Yes." She looked up at him, those huge eyes even wider. "I'm the only Colby Agency employee here. I can't just pretend nothing's happening up there."

Technically he was almost a Colby Agency employee. But that would all be over by light of day. Maybe she was right. Maybe foiling these guys' plan was the right thing to do.

An explosion thundered overhead. East side of the building.

"What the hell?" He got to his feet and barely missed whacking his head against a steel beam. From the sound of that explosion some things might very well be over way before tomorrow.

"Where did that come from?" She was right beside him, huddled close.

"Elevator shaft."

"Why would they blow up the elevator shaft?"

He exhaled a heavy breath. "They're not. They're blowing the doors open."

"Why? The elevators aren't going to work with the power out."

"They're not trying to get them to work."

He had a pretty good idea what they were up to.

"Gibson." She glared at him when he shifted his attention from the elevator shafts to her. "Explain what the hell you're talking about."

"They're not trying to blow anything up, Elaine. They're looking for you or us, if they've figured out I'm here, too. Hiding in an elevator shaft is the oldest trick in the book. They do it all the time in the movies. They're probably going to cover the whole building."

She moved away from him a little as if she didn't want to be too close in the event his reasoning was contagious. "How can you be so sure that's what they're doing? Maybe they're trying to get those cases up the elevator. That's what they were in the middle of doing when the power went out."

He shook his head, ignored her pleading look. "I don't think so. I think they want to make sure we don't get out of here."

"Wait a minute," she all but shouted.

He shot her a warning look. "Are you trying to tip them off?" he asked in a growl of a whisper.

"Sorry." She took a deep breath. "What I'm trying to say is, why would they want to kill us? I mean, other than for the obvious—if we get in their way or what not. As long as they get what they came for, what do they care if they get us or not? It's not like we can identify them. Maybe whatever they're doing has nothing to do with us."

He was going to have to tell her. There was no way around it. He hoped like hell she would still be cooperative after this. Of course he couldn't be absolutely positive they were looking for him or her, but considering the trouble he was in he was pretty damned sure he was the reason they were here. It wasn't totally outside the realm of possibility that an enemy of the Colby Agency could be the reason as well, but he'd wager this was about him.

"This may not have anything to do with the Colby Agency," he admitted.

Confusion made one tiny line across her forehead and showed up in the way of dimples in her cheeks as her lips pursed. Why the hell hadn't they met under different circumstances? He was drawn to so many things about her.

"You're talking but you're telling me nothing again," she said ruefully. "It feels like you're not being completely honest."

He was made. Confession time.

"Three months ago—"

Another explosion rent the air.

Elaine crowded against him. "Another elevator door?" The worry in her eyes tugged at his protective instincts.

"I don't think so. That sounded different." There was always the chance those men had come here to destroy the entire building just to make sure no evidence was left behind at Welton Investments. Unfortunately, if the building went down, they went down. "Stay put," he told Elaine. "I'm going to check this out."

"No way. I'm going with you."

"I can move faster alone." She couldn't argue that. But she did. "I'll keep up."

More scraping, twisting sounds echoed from somewhere overhead. He needed to move now. He had to know what they were up to. The second floor was where Welton Investments offices were housed. Where the evidence he needed was.

"All right, but if you can't keep up I'll have to stash you somewhere."

"I'll keep up."

Her determination only served to increase his admiration for her. What a shame. He finally met a woman he truly admired and he was on the verge of a lengthy jail sentence, if not death.

Life just wasn't fair.

He surveyed the space between floors that sprawled before them. The majority of the sound had come from the area around the elevator shafts. What he needed was to get above that position so that he could look down through a ventilation grill or something. He'd just have to figure out that part as he went.

Moving cautiously across the maze of beams, he made his way to the elevator shafts. Elaine stayed right behind him every step of the way. She wasn't as agile as he was, but she handled herself damned well.

Between the two elevator shafts that ran straight up through the building, all the way to the roof, was part of the ventilation system, as well as a stationary ladder used to access various points in the elevator shafts.

Might as well start there.

When he reached the ladder, he turned to her. "Do you want to go first?" He gestured to the ladder.

She looked at him skeptically. "Now you're the one who's kidding, right?" One hand smoothed over her skirt as a reminder.

"Oh, yeah. I forgot about that." And he had. He'd

struggled to keep his eyes closed when he'd lifted her through the ceiling. Only once did he peek. He hadn't meant to, but some evil gene had forced one eye open a crack. He'd watched her come and go from this building for a long time and she generally wore darker colors or what one would call earth tones. But there was nothing earth-toned about her panties. Hot, sassy pink.

She gestured for him to precede her.

"Stay close," he cautioned.

"Don't worry. I'm not letting you out of my sight for anything. You're the one who knows how to get us back out of here."

He headed up the ladder. The floor above the current position of the interlopers was his destination. He needed an access for the ventilation system. Going up through that ductwork might just be impossible, but coming down was another story. If he could get above them, he could keep an eye on what they were up to.

Checking Elaine's progress as he went made for slower going, but he had to be sure she didn't lose her balance or get into trouble. If she ever started looking down that was when any problems with fear would show up. Some people lived the biggest part of their lives without realizing they were afraid of heights. Then, some unexpected event would put them in a position much like this and bam, acrophobia.

A few more wrungs and they would be past the

second floor. He reached that level and listened. Whatever they were doing it was definitely on that floor.

His floor.

Maybe this intrusion hadn't been about breaking into the Colby Agency or even eliminating him. The fact that the intruders had used the musicians hired by the Colby Agency for access to the building might strictly be opportunity and nothing more. The real musicians could be out there in the parking lot dead.

As far as getting to him, he'd just figured that when they didn't get him at his apartment they'd come here looking for him under the assumption that this was the place he'd come back to, the scene of the crime so to speak. And they would have assumed right. He'd waited until everyone was gone to come in. He'd had a plan of his own…but things had gone awry when the first security guard went down.

He may or may not be the target at this point. Maybe they hadn't come here looking for him at all.

The files. His only evidence that could prove his innocence.

He'd taken the risk of coming back here tonight to retrieve those files. He'd known that searching his apartment would be their first move when he didn't come back to work. So he'd hidden his evidence at the firm. All he had to do was get back in and get it.

Not a problem.

Except now it looked as if someone had beaten him to the punch. Someone had come up with the same idea.

While he'd been waiting for the opportunity to slip past the guard, these guys had moved in. He had known his name would be on the "do not allow entrance" list at this point. Without that evidence he'd compiled it would only be his word against the firm's. The firm would win since they had likely doctored files to point guilt at him. But he had copies of the original files. He felt certain a good forensics expert could tell the difference.

A third explosion rattled the very walls of the elevator shafts. The ladder shook.

A muffled scream echoed from below him.

He looked down just in time to witness Elaine losing her grip on the ladder.

Chapter Five

10:31 p.m.

Slow motion.

She was falling in slow motion.

Somehow her right hand snagged a passing rung.

The abrupt stop of her body's tumble snapped at her shoulder…and it felt as if the joint ripped right out of its socket.

Some animalistic instinct for survival had her groping with her left hand. She couldn't get her feet to work or she'd grab on with those, too.

Her lungs felt ready to explode. Her heart threatened to burst out of her chest.

She didn't know how much farther she had to fall, but she understood that she wouldn't survive.

Looking down wasn't an option.

Her brain told her legs to wrap around the ladder.

Anything to take the weight off her throbbing shoulder. Why wouldn't her legs work?

Her right foot hooked onto a rung and her entire body quivered with relief.

Thank God. Thank God.

"Don't move."

Gibson was just above her.

She'd almost forgotten him.

"Elaine, focus, okay? Don't let go and don't move."

Was he insane? Why would she let go? It was a long way down there. Not to mention she'd crash through that ceiling and fall a few more feet if a steel beam didn't stop her fall first.

"I'm not moving." Why was he looking at her like that?

Something in his eyes told her she was wrong but that didn't make sense. She was holding on to the ladder with both hands. And one foot.

What did he see that she didn't?

That was when she made her next mistake.

She looked down.

Something red flowed swiftly down her left leg.

What in the world?

It dripped off her little toe and got lost in the air as it plunged downward. She blinked. The steel beams and wires and tiles moved beneath her. Started to fade in and out of focus.

Her fingers felt numb...didn't want to work anymore.

Bile burned at the back of her throat.

What was wrong with her?

"Elaine, look at me!"

She couldn't do what he said.

Why the hell was she bleeding?

At that precise moment she knew only one thing for certain.

She couldn't hold on any longer.

As if watching someone else's hand, she saw her fingers release the rung. First her left hand… then her right.

But she didn't fall.

Strong fingers had latched around her right wrist.

She stared up at Gibson. He pulled her toward him. How could he be that strong? That fast? Or maybe he was moving down toward her while holding on to her. She wasn't sure. Her mind wouldn't work right.

"Grab on to the ladder, Elaine," he commanded.

She made the fingers of her free hand curl around the closest rung once more. She was cold. Really cold. Her skin felt weird…clammy and sticky.

She closed her eyes. Tried to stop the spinning in her head.

He was next to her then, next to her and all around her at the same time. She felt his arm go around her waist. "Put your arms around my neck. Do it *now*, Elaine."

She heard him but she couldn't open her eyes. Somehow her arms did as he'd commanded.

They were moving. She couldn't stand the motion. Her stomach roiled. She wanted to warn him that she might be sick but her mouth wouldn't work.

Suddenly she was on the floor…maybe one of those platforms like they'd been on before. She couldn't remember.

The room still spun. The ladder kept flying around but she wasn't on the ladder anymore so she didn't care.

Fabric ripped and she made her head move to see what Gibson was doing now. He'd torn one of the sleeves from his shirt and was wrapping it around her leg.

More of the ripping sound and his other sleeve ended up wrapped around her thigh, too.

The spinning started to slow. She managed to raise up onto her elbows. Just in time to roll onto her right side and puke like a dog who'd wolfed down too much too fast.

When she'd stopped heaving, she laid back and squeezed her eyes shut for a moment. Her head ached. Her shoulder throbbed like a son of a gun. She knew her leg should hurt but right now it didn't…not really.

"How you doing?"

Her eyes opened and she found Gibson leaning over her. "I don't know. What happened?"

He seemed uncertain for a moment. "There was anther explosion and you fell. Somehow you cut your leg." He glanced up at the ladder. "Something on the ladder probably."

His description set off a torrent of pain in her leg. She grimaced. "Yeah, I'm feeling that now." She rubbed at her mouth. "What about the dizziness and…" She started to shrug but her shoulder burned like hellfire itself. "I felt dizzy and clammy and numb."

"Panic maybe."

He checked her leg. His fingers felt cool against the stinging flesh. "I don't think the damage is serious."

She remembered seeing the blood run down her leg. "I didn't like damage an artery or anything, did I?"

"No. The bleeding has slowed considerably. Still…" He sat back on his haunches. "You need a patch job."

Oh, damn. "Well, I guess I'm pretty much screwed." It wasn't like those masked bastards would let them out of here to get her leg sewn up.

"Is there an emergency first aid kit on your floor?"

"Sure." Fat lot of good it was doing them here. "In the lounge in the cupboard over the sink."

"Those the keys to that floor?"

She'd forgotten about having the ring of keys on her wrist. It was a miracle she hadn't lost them the way she had her boots and tights. She couldn't even remember where she'd left them at this point. Apparently, she'd instinctively held on to them so they wouldn't rattle. Otherwise the jingle would have reminded her she'd been wearing them. "Yeah."

"I'll go for the first-aid kit and come back."

Her brain might still be a little fuzzy but she knew what that meant.

"No way, Gibson. It's too dangerous. You've got the bleeding under control. Let's just ride it out right here until morning."

He seemed to consider her strategy for a moment then he shook his head.

"No can do. If you have to move…"

He didn't have to say the rest. The bad guys could show, which would force her to move. The gash must be pretty bad for him to be this concerned. The memory of blood slipping down her leg inserted itself in front of all other thoughts.

"I'm not so sure there's any sewing paraphernalia in the first-aid kit." That was true. Why take this risk only to bring back a few bandages and ointment?

She'd be a whole lot happier if he stayed right here with her. A whole lot happier.

"No one in your agency keeps a sewing kit around?"

She closed her eyes and settled back onto the floor or whatever the hell it was. There was no point in debating with him. He'd made up his mind.

"There's a sewing kit in Mildred's office," she said, too weary to really talk. "In the top center drawer of the credenza. She doesn't lock it."

"All right." He reached for the ring of keys on her wrist. "Walk me through the keys I'll need."

She showed him the stairwell door key first. The key to the lounge if by some off chance it was locked. It hadn't been earlier, but if anyone had closed the door, who knew?

"Don't move and don't make any noise," he ordered.

"Don't worry." She'd just lay right here with her bloody leg and the stench of vomit and count her blessings.

He squeezed her right hand. "I'll be back as quickly as possible."

That was the one thing in all this she didn't worry about. He'd be back or die trying. Funny how she knew that and she'd scarcely known the man an hour.

BRAD LISTENED above the first-floor ladies' room for at least a minute before he moved the tile. He eased down onto the still closed toilet seat and then slid the ceiling tile back into place.

Again he listened, just to make sure he was alone in the ladies' room.

It had been a long time since he'd played a game like this, he considered as he leaned against the door and listened for any sound in the corridor beyond.

Not since he was a kid playing hide-and-seek with his cousins at holiday get-togethers.

Slowly, his senses on the highest state of alert, he

eased the door open. He took a deep, bolstering breath before stepping out into the corridor.

Clear.

Once in the corridor he moved swiftly. He turned all the way around twice before reaching the stairwell door and without slowing his forward advancement.

He had to hurry.

He slid the key into the stairwell door and opened it. Again he took his time at this point, listening, watching. When he was sure he was alone in the stairwell, he allowed the door to close behind him.

Taking the stairs two at a time he reached the fourth floor in record time. He'd climbed this route several times in the past few weeks for his interview sessions. He wondered if this would be the last time.

He didn't hear any sound beyond the entry door that would lead onto the fourth floor.

Again he used the key and let himself pass the next barrier.

He remembered where the lounge was located. He'd certainly passed by it enough times. The first-aid kit was right where she'd said it would be. He grabbed a couple of bottles of water out of the fridge, too.

Crackers might be good since Elaine had gotten ill. He prowled quickly through the cupboards until he found a box of snack crackers. He shoved a couple of packages into his trouser pockets.

He checked the first-aid kit—no sewing supplies, only butterfly bandages.

Easing to the door he stood very still and listened for any noise that wasn't him breathing.

Silence flowed down the long corridor.

He slipped out of the lounge, keeping his movements slow and soundless.

He paused in Mildred's office to locate the sewing kit in the credenza. When he had everything he thought he'd need he headed back to the stairwell. The travel-size sewing kit was in his back pocket. A bottle of water and a pack of crackers filled each front pocket. The first-aid kit was tucked beneath his left arm.

Once back in the stairwell, he paused long enough to ensure he was still alone before flying down the stairs. At the first floor, he went through the usual routine of ensuring no one was in the corridor beyond the stairwell door.

He'd made it back into the ladies' room before he took a deep breath. He checked his watch and grimaced at how long he'd taken to get back.

Four more minutes were required to reach the location where he'd left Elaine. When he first approached her she looked so still that fear closed his throat.

But then she stirred. Her eyes opened and he relaxed.

"You doing okay?" He knelt next to her.

"Don't ask stupid questions, Gibson."

Sounded as if she were on the road to recovery already.

He opened a bottle of the water and helped her drink. He thought about offering her the crackers but he figured he'd better wait until the leg was taken care of first.

After opening the first-aid kit he deliberated on what he had to work with. Antibacterial ointment, gauze and tape. Scissors. Wound-cleansing pads. In the sewing kit there were half a dozen needles of varying sizes and several small collections of thread. He picked the one that appeared to be more nylon than cotton and set it aside. The black color wouldn't have been his first choice but that wasn't the primary objective. He needed strength.

"Let me ask you a question, Gibson."

He smiled, adding a measure of reassurance for her benefit. "Ask away." Hopefully it wouldn't have anything to do with his former career.

"Have you ever sewn anything?"

Her dubious tone was backed up by her expression. She'd had time to think about it and she was worried. Not that he could blame her. Though the bleeding appeared to be under control, this was a hell of a gaping wound. He wondered again what had snagged her.

"Believe it or not, I have."

Her gaze narrowed. "What? A hole in your sock?"

He couldn't ever remember sharing this with anyone who wasn't related to him. And he hadn't exactly shared it then. His family had simply known what he did every summer.

"I've patched up a number of dogs and cats. One horse. Oh, yes, and one ferret. I spent my summers in high school helping out at a local vet clinic."

She smiled but the expression looked more like a grimace. "Is that supposed to make me feel better?"

No. Nothing about this would make her feel better. It was going to hurt like hell.

"We need to get this done. I can't be sure how much longer we'll be safe here. The fourth floor was clear and I haven't heard anything in the past few minutes but that doesn't mean they aren't looking for us."

"Yeah, yeah, I get it." She wrapped her arms over her chest. "I guess I'm ready."

Brad used the cleaning pads to sterilize his hands as best he could, as well as one of the needles.

Taking his time he unwrapped the injury. He felt her tense as the fabric, sticky with blood, pulled away from the wound. This wasn't going to be pleasant by any stretch of the imagination.

Blood started to ooze again but he dabbed at it with clean gauze. "Brace for a sting," he warned before dabbing a fresh cleansing pad over the injured area. Her left leg stiffened.

The tear was about three inches in width and was about ten inches above her knee.

This would take some time.

He placed her hand against his thigh. "Feel free to pinch the crap out of me if it makes you feel any better."

"I don't think that's going to help but thanks for the thought."

Clanging inside the elevator shaft behind them sent a new wave of tension through him.

Their gazes met and he saw the fear in hers. "Just get it over with, Gibson."

He threaded the needle and tied a firm knot in the end. He dabbed the wound again and did what he had to do.

With each prick of the needle she tensed, then quivered, but she never uttered a sound. Not one.

He made the stitches small and close. Sweat beaded on his forehead and rolled down his back. By the time he'd completed the last stitch his hands had started to shake.

"That's it."

He felt her relax. Her eyes were closed against the pain but tears had poured from the corners. The idea of how much pain she'd endured made him sick to his stomach.

He covered the injury in clean gauze he'd slickened with ointment to prevent it from sticking. With that bandage taped into place, he wrapped more gauze around her thigh tightly enough to give the wound some additional support, then he taped that as well.

She sat up as soon as he'd finished, careful to keep her leg still. "I guess it could've been worse."

More admiration welled inside him. She was a trooper.

"Then again, you didn't let me see it. It could be all Frankensteinish."

He reached into his pocket and removed a pack of the crumbled snack crackers. "Here. Eat." He pulled out the other pack and forced himself to eat. They both needed something inside their stomachs besides the bitter fear and uncertainty of what was going on outside this rudimentary hiding place.

"What do we do now?"

He knew what he wanted to do, but he wasn't sure he wanted to attempt it again with her injured leg. And he damned sure couldn't leave her here.

"Don't tell me." She looked up at the ladder looming high above their heads. "I think you're trying to do me in, Gibson."

"I'm relatively sure this isn't about the Colby Agency. I think it's about my firm…and me."

She took a long swallow of water and swiped the back of her hand across her mouth. "Am I going to get the whole story now?"

Why not? She'd earned it. "About three months ago I noticed some discrepancies in various accounts."

"Discrepancies like missing money or other assets?"

He nodded. "Something like that. It's a little more complicated but that's the idea."

"Did you tell anyone?"

"Not at first." This was where he'd really gone stupid. "I'm just a junior associate. I figured I'd better have all my facts straight before I started accusing a senior partner of anything illegal."

"I hope you kept records of what you found."

She could see where this was going.

"Yeah. I documented every single item. Then I went to the top of the heap with my findings."

"And the illegal activities went all the way to the top."

He rubbed the back of his neck, fought the exhaustion. "All the way to the top. I just didn't know it until about forty-eight hours ago."

"You think that's why these guys are here?"

He rested his gaze on hers. "I think so." Nothing he could say would be apology enough for dragging her into this ugly mess.

"You could be right," she allowed. "But that still doesn't explain why the men after you used the Colby Agency to get in." She looked up toward the fourth floor. "We need to know who they are and why they're here. It's the only way we can protect our respective assets. If those men are here about your predicament, then there must be something on the second floor they expect to find. Same goes for the fourth floor, if it's about the Colby Agency."

He explained his theory about the men using the arriving musicians as an opportunity for access. She agreed that it was a possibility.

"I still say we have to find out what they're up to."

"I'm not sure you can handle what we might have to do with that injured leg."

She struggled to her feet, refused to let him help, then winced when her full weight came down on her legs. "I can handle whatever I have to." She lifted her chin and glowered at him defiantly. "What about you, you up to this?"

"This time," he countered without acknowledging her dig as to whether he was up to it or not, "we go up together."

She turned to the ladder. "Whatever. Let's just do it. I want to know what these bastards are doing up there."

They moved up the ladder, slowly, painfully slowly. He stayed pinned against her back, his feet just one rung beneath hers. His hands only inches above hers.

They'd almost reached the third floor when he discovered the culprit that had ripped open her thigh. A broken, rusty eye hook that had been a part of the ladder's original design. Probably used as part of a hoist. The blood clinging to the rusty protrusion confirmed his suspicions.

"You had a tetanus shot lately?"

"A couple of years ago."

"Good."

Funny, he'd dated a number of women in the past. Some for a few months, others only once. He knew more about this woman in just a couple of hours than he'd known about any of the other women he'd ever dated.

"Okay. This is our stop."

He assisted her onto a beam above the second floor. The same dropped ceiling would provide access when the time was right.

Stealth was particularly important now. A single sound could have them dancing around gunfire.

His first objective was to determine exactly where the intruders were. Once he'd deemed it safe, he would drop down into his colleague's office and retrieve the file. He'd hidden it in Darren Turner's office rather than his own. Turner was new and loud. None of the others liked him and the chances of him participating in anything criminal were slim to none. Even if he found the file, he wouldn't know how to access it.

Elaine tugged on his shirt. He froze. Listened to the voices below.

A disagreement had erupted between what sounded like three men. Where was number four?

"They can't leave this building," one commanded.

Well that was clear enough. Behind him, Elaine tensed.

"Get it done," the same man snarled. "I don't care if it takes all night. Then we'll take care of those loose ends."

Brad waited. He listened as the men set about going from office to office. At least they hadn't found his file so far. That was something. He had one last chance here. He had to get his hands on that file first. In his opinion, there was no question now why these men were here.

If he hadn't weakened that one time and told the senior partner about the file, he wouldn't be in this position right now. But he'd trusted the man. That had been his first mistake.

His former boss knew everything there was to know about him. He'd used that knowledge to frame Brad. Without that evidence he couldn't prove his story.

He needed that file.

He'd worked months to collect it. The idea that he could go down for what those greedy bastards had done made him want to roar with fury.

Elaine tugged on his shirt again.

He leaned down close where she could whisper in his ear.

"I hate to do this to you, Gibson, but I really have to go to the bathroom."

"How long can you wait?" He needed more time to ensure those men were out of hearing range before they made a move.

"Maybe two minutes."

If she hadn't looked so distressed he might have challenged her to hold out. But she'd been through an awful lot already. She deserved a break.

All he had to do was find the restroom. He'd been to it a thousand times but everything looked different from up here. He'd just have to use trial and error.

He located the bathroom in record time. Listening to ensure the coast was clear, he then slid a ceiling tile aside. He climbed down onto the toilet in the stall on the end. Then he helped Elaine down. He shimmied the tile back into place and stepped off the toilet seat.

"Make it fast," he murmured. They couldn't risk getting caught. He slid the lock into place for the good that would do against a killer with a gun.

"You don't expect me to do it right here, do you?"

"Just hurry, okay?"

He turned his back fully to her, giving her some semblance of the privacy she wanted. She just stood there for a moment then she huffed out a breath of sound and wiggled her flashy pink panties down. He heard the silky fabric drag along her skin.

The mere idea of how nicely rounded her derriere was had the blood pooling in a region other than his brain.

She took care of her business, then they swapped places and he took care of his. She was right. This was more than a little awkward when you were on the relieving end.

He caught himself before he flushed the toilet.

"Okay, let's get back up there." The longer they stayed down here the more likely they were to be caught. He needed to consider his next move very carefully.

He climbed onto the toilet seat and extended her a hand to join him.

He'd just reached for the tile he intended to move when the door leading into the room opened.

Acting on instinct, he hunkered down in the nearest thing to a crouch he could manage with her tucked solidly against his back, both of them balancing on the toilet.

The door leading into the restroom swept closed.

The whisper of rubber soles on ceramic tile paused near the row of sinks.

What he would give for a weapon. He'd never fired one in his life, but he would damn sure try.

The sound of the door to the first stall opening riveted his attention to a new level of absolute fear.

No way were they getting out of here without trouble.

Chapter Six

11:45 p.m.
The home of Lucas and Victoria Colby-Camp

Victoria stepped back and studied her Christmas tree.
Lucas had put the tree up a week ago, but she'd
wanted to wait until tonight to decorate it. The ever-
green scent had filled her home as the tree acclimated
to its new environment, fueling her anticipation.
She'd been anxious to load down its limbs with red
velvet and gold satin ribbons, and glistening glass
balls in the jewel tones she loved so well.

She hadn't expected to decorate it alone.

Lucas's flight had been delayed. They had both
known by six this evening that the chances of him
getting home tonight were not good, but they had
hoped. If all went well he would be home before
noon tomorrow.

He should have taken her up on her offer to send

the agency jet for him before it was too late. The
airports on the east coast were seriously backed up
now. Not even any of the usual private airfields were
able to take in any more arrivals.

She hung the last of the glittering snowflakes in
place. At least Lucas was here in spirit.

A pleased smile spread across her lips. The tree was
beautiful. Her husband and family would approve.

As she packed up the ornament boxes and stored
them away in the guestroom closet, a niggling sense
of disquiet began to build. She told herself it was
because Lucas hadn't made it home, but she wasn't
at all sure that was the case.

It was too late to call her son. But if anything had
gone wrong, she would know it by now. No question
Jim would call her.

Still, she felt a mounting uneasiness. She walked
over to the front window and stared out at the thick-
ening blanket of snow. Perhaps the prospect that the
airports would close entirely and Lucas would be
stuck in D.C. for Christmas had set off the increas-
ing tension she felt.

Perhaps hot cocoa would lighten her mood. She
padded to the kitchen, admiring the recent changes
to her home. She and Lucas had bought this house
right after their marriage. The neighborhood was
gated and plenty elegant for anyone's taste. As with
any home one didn't build from the ground up,

there were changes she'd wanted to make. The last of the renovations had been completed just before Thanksgiving.

Besides the typical cosmetic changes such as carpeting and painting, they'd opened up the entry foyer, introducing a soaring cathedral ceiling. They'd also added new hardwood throughout the downstairs and lovely new kitchen cabinets, counters and appliances.

She and Lucas had furnished the home with a combination of their lifelong accumulations, which ensured an eclectic, appealing décor.

Everything was perfect. Exactly as it should be.

Then why the lingering feelings of uncertainty tonight? She poured milk into a stainless steel pan and set it atop the stove. A gentle twist of the right knob and the flames jumped to life beneath it.

Things were going extremely well at the agency. The renovations had been completed there this year as well. Clients commented frequently that the décor was sophisticated yet welcoming. The younger investigators who had been added to the staff this year kept a sense of excitement and a raw power simmering in every staff meeting. She just couldn't see how it could get any better, at home or at work.

Her life was all, and more, than she could ever have hoped for.

The milk warmed and she slowly added the sugar and cocoa to taste. After stirring thoroughly, she poured the warm brew into her favorite mug and went to the living room to enjoy her newly decorated tree.

Despite the pleasant taste of the cocoa, she couldn't get past the idea that something was very wrong. She'd sensed these things before and whenever the feelings were this powerful the events to follow were usually devastating.

She wished she could shake the gloom. If anything was wrong, someone would have called her by now. Yet, putting the troubling thoughts aside didn't work.

The urge to get dressed and go into the office was nearly overwhelming. It just didn't make sense. She'd been running the Colby Agency for more than twenty years, things were better now than ever before. There was absolutely no logical reason for her to feel this way.

The doorbell chimed.

Her heart reacted to the unexpected sound.

She set her mug aside and stood, her pulse racing with the idea that Jim might have had to take Tasha to the hospital. But wouldn't he have simply called?

The faces and names of all those who kept the Colby Agency thriving flickered past her mind's eyes, escalating her tension and tugging at her heart. She prayed there was nothing wrong.

This was Christmas.

A time for peace and happiness.

She peered through the peephole, but couldn't see anything but a huge bundle—it was far too large to call a bouquet—of red roses.

What on earth?

What floral shop delivered at this time of night?

Before opening the door, she readied to press the panic button on her home security system. The keypad was right next to the door. Security would be here in under two minutes. Surely if this were trouble, she could fend it off for that long.

But what kind of trouble came bearing armloads of roses?

Time to find out.

One hand at the security keypad, she opened the door. Before she could demand to see a face, the flowers were lowered slightly and Lucas smiled mischievously over the top of the lush blooms. Victoria's heart took an ardent leap while her mouth opened wide in disbelief.

"Santa decided to come a little early," he teased. "He gave me a lift in his sleigh."

She couldn't believe it! He was home!

The cold wind bit at her through the silk robe she wore. She grabbed Lucas by the coat sleeve. "Get in here."

When he'd kicked the snow off his shoes and stepped inside, she closed the door behind him to shut out the wind.

"Where did you get all these roses?" He had at least five dozen.

He winked. "I know people."

Well, he was right about that. Lucas Camp probably had an inside track with the Almighty Himself.

"Let me have those." She took the roses into her arms. The smell was heavenly. "You get out of those damp clothes."

She didn't question him further on how he'd managed a flight to Chicago. He had friends in high places…and other places he didn't readily talk about. She didn't care how he got home. She was only glad that he was here.

Filling three vases to overflowing, she placed one on the dining room table, another in the living room and the final one in the entry hall. She'd woven a bit of gold ribbon through the stems and around the vase to add a holiday touch. Very nice. A tingle of excitement started low in her belly at how very much she loved her husband. That he would take the time to bring her roses at this time of night just because he was late made her heart flutter. He was truly one of a kind.

Before he joined her in the living room clad in his favorite pajamas and a thick, luxuriant robe, she made him a cup of hot cocoa to chase away the chill.

He settled on the sofa next to her and drank deeply from his mug. "Hmmm. Now that hits the spot."

She placed a hand on his leg and squeezed. "Thank you for making it home tonight."

He turned to her, the heartfelt emotion in his eyes making her yearn to be in his arms. "I wouldn't have missed this moment for the world." He placed a chaste kiss on her forehead. "Nice tree, by the way."

Her gaze moved back to the tree. "Yes, it is a lovely tree."

Victoria relaxed. All was well now. Lucas was home and when she glanced at the clock, she saw it was officially Christmas Eve.

She refused to let that unreasonable anxiety take root again. Everything was fine.

Everything was exactly as it should be.

Chapter Seven

Inside the Colby Agency

Elaine didn't dare breathe.

Her heart pounded at the speed of light.

Her legs trembled with the effort of holding up her weight in this awkward semicrouching position, one foot on either side of the toilet seat. This one didn't have a lid. Gibson was perched on the toilet with her, his backside glued to her front. He was probably the only reason she'd stayed vertical like this for the past minute, that felt far more like a century.

Her tightly clenched teeth were all that kept her from groaning out loud with the pain shooting up her left thigh. The man with the gun was at the stall door right in front of them. The crackers she'd eaten minutes ago felt like crushed glass in her stomach. The door bumped against the lock as the man on the other side pushed first, then reached up and grabbed the top of the door to yank it open. The flimsy slide lock resisted, kept the door from opening immediately. But that wouldn't last.

His knees creaked. Elaine's gaze dropped to the floor. He'd squatted down to take a look under the door.

Terror mushroomed all over again.

He would see them.

As she watched in abject horror, Gibson reached out, seemingly in slow motion, and slid the lock to the open position. Then, his movements launching into high speed, he executed this jump-kick thing where he hurled himself upward and at the door, slamming the slab of metal into the crouched man's face and sending him reeling backward.

Elaine held on to the wall, shock preventing her from moving. Her bare toes gripped the cold porcelain bowl beneath her as if she feared it might fly right out from under her in the next two seconds.

The two men rolled around on the floor, a seemingly solid black mass of a figure fighting ferociously against Gibson's leaner, khaki-and-striped-clad frame.

A glint of black metal in the thug's hand sucked the air out of her lungs.

His weapon.

He would kill Gibson.

She had to do something.

She jumped off the toilet, grimaced at the pain that speared from knee to hip. Doing her best not to trip over the legs of the man who now had Gibson pinned to the ground, she all but fell out of the stall.

Frantically surveying the restroom, she found nothing she could use as a weapon.

What could she do now?

Gibson's arm shook with the effort of holding the man's weapon away from his face.

Damn.

She had to do something fast.

First rule of female fighting as best she remembered it from back in high school: go for the hair. She jerked off the guy's mask and dug both hands into his sweaty locks. As she pulled with all her might, he lost the upper hand on Gibson as he fought to jerk loose from her hold.

She pulled harder.

He tried to knock her out of the way with his right elbow but she was practically straddling his trunk with his shoulders arched backwards so the move didn't work.

Gibson jammed the heel of his hand beneath the guy's chin. The gun clattered to the floor. Gibson shoved him onto his back, almost bowling Elaine over in the process. Now Gibson was on top, but the man had him by the throat.

The gun.

She needed the gun.

Elaine scrambled past the struggling men and snatched up the abandoned weapon.

"Stop it!" She almost bit her tongue off when she remembered she shouldn't be shouting. Taking a steadying breath, she held the gun the way she'd seen cops do it on *Law and Order*.

Gibson was the first to notice, but didn't bother heeding her demand. He was too busy banging the guy's head against the floor and trying to rear back from the reach of his clutching hands.

She tried her best not to point the weapon at Gibson, but it was difficult to avoid him with all the movement. Her throat was dry. Her leg hurt like hell and her palms were sweating. The gun started to shake in her hands and she knew she was in trouble.

Okay, this wasn't working.

She flattened against the wall and scooted past the two, putting herself at the bad guy's head. She held the weapon down where he couldn't possibly miss it pointed at his face. Gibson abruptly noticed and looked up at her.

"I said, stop it." She pressed the business end of the weapon against the man's forehead when he continued to struggle. Oh, yeah, this was a lot better.

The man stilled instantly. That was more like it.

"Give me the weapon."

The sharp demand made her jump, almost ticked her off, but Gibson was right. She didn't even know if it was on safety or had a safety. She wondered if he did.

She gave him the weapon.

He kept it aimed at the guy while he dug around in the man's pockets. "Let's just see who you are."

Elaine licked her lips, tried to calm herself. Her heart still pounded like crazy. The urge to run was a palpable force surging through her veins. But, like Gibson, she desperately wanted to know what the hell was going on.

"Why are you here?" Gibson demanded, mindful, unlike her, of the need to keep quiet.

"You don't want to know the answer to that," the man snarled.

Elaine wanted to kick him in the head, but she was barefoot so she didn't. He was in no position at the moment to be so mean and uncooperative.

Gibson moved his free hand over the guy, checking for other weapons, she presumed.

"Where're your friends?" he asked next.

"Close," the guy said smugly. "You and your friend don't have a chance. We have our orders."

"Well, then," Gibson said, "*your friends* are going to be very disappointed in you." Gibson glanced up at her. "Take off his boots."

Though she couldn't fathom why he'd asked her to do such a thing, the dead serious look in his eyes told her he wasn't kidding.

He gagged the guy using his own socks, then Gibson rolled him onto his belly and used the guy's own belt as well as his boot laces to secure his hands and feet together behind his back. Didn't look comfortable. Looked even less escapable.

Gibson snagged the radio the man had carried and passed it to Elaine. "We may need that." He checked for any other usable gear. A second clip for the weapon was the only other item he took.

Voices in the corridor outside the door shifted the attention of everyone in the restroom in that direction and sent panic searing through Elaine's veins.

Thank God Gibson had the presence of mind to keep the weapon pressed to the forehead of the man on the floor. Otherwise she was certain he would have started grunting and growling for attention.

At least two men passed without pausing.

When she'd counted to ten and they hadn't come back, Elaine sagged with relief.

"Hold this."

She turned to Gibson. He thrust the gun in her direction. "What're you doing now?"

"I'm going to stick our friend here in the stall so he won't be readily noticeable if anyone pokes his head in the door."

"Good idea."

Dang. Gibson was pretty smart for a money man. He kind of reminded her of the guys at the agency. He'd definitely gotten her vote of confidence over the course of the past couple of hours. Her shoulder and leg ached, reminding her of the extent to which he'd gone to in order to take care of her.

No one, outside her family, had ever gone that far out of their way for her before. That made him a nice guy in her book. A really nice guy.

He scooted their prisoner into the stall and pushed the door closed. Elaine waited at the entry door. She had to hand it to Gibson, that last move was a really good idea. She had to kind of hunker down to see the guy in the far stall. Hopefully anyone who peeked inside this restroom would overlook him entirely. Unless he started making a lot of noise. They couldn't do much more about that short of killing him and neither of them were prepared to go there unless self-defense necessitated extreme force.

Just tying him up would hopefully buy them some additional time.

For what, she didn't exactly know.

Except maybe to stay alive.

They were armed now. That was something. Her gaze settled on the weapon as Gibson tucked it into his waistband at the small of his back.

She had the radio, though she wasn't sure what they needed it for. Contacting the other bad guys was not on her agenda.

When Gibson joined her at the door, she asked, "You don't think we need to attempt to interrogate him any further?" Gibson had asked him a couple of questions, but he'd refused to answer.

Gibson leaned in close to her and spoke for her ears only. "I don't think it'll do any good and, frankly, we need to get out of here before his friends come looking for him. Luck may not stay with us much longer."

She nodded. "Gotcha."

Maybe the need to uncover relevant facts was rubbing off on her. The building was under siege, it would be nice to know why beyond all doubt.

Gibson was pretty sure this attack was about him and the evidence he'd uncovered at Welton Investments, but Elaine wasn't so sure. Why had these guys gone to the fourth floor when they first arrived? Why had they pretended to be the entertainment for the Colby Agency Christmas party? Sure, Gibson could be right about that part. These guys could have used those musicians as a means of entrance and they could have gone straight to the fourth floor looking for her, but that didn't rule anything out to her way of thinking.

Maybe she had worked for a private investigations agency too long to give the benefit of the doubt so freely, but wouldn't guys like the one they'd just bound and gagged have a plan way before they arrived on the scene?

From the looks of things these men were professionals. They wouldn't just show up and wait for an opportunity. They would make their own opportunities.

"I'll make sure the coast is clear."

She nodded. If Gibson had any experience whatsoever in stealth, he had more than her.

Leaning against the wall next to the door kept the weight off her leg. She didn't look forward to running. Hopefully she wouldn't have to.

Gibson drew the door inward, little by little, then eased just as gradually into the corridor. When she heard no running footsteps or shouted warning from him, she followed using the same caution.

The corridor wasn't as well lit as the ones on the fourth floor. Then she saw why. Some of the emergency lights were dark. Very strange. Was the whole building being neglected by maintenance? In her opinion the lockdown thing was dangerous to anyone who might get trapped in the building. She'd cut her leg on that elevator shaft ladder. And now this. Complaints definitely would be filed.

Assuming she survived this night.

Gibson led her along the corridor until they reached an intersection. He hesitated a moment and listened. She did the same. She had no desire to run into any more of those men. The short nap carpet felt good under her feet after all that time on the beams and the ladder.

She shuddered when she considered that she'd spent serious time in bathrooms without any shoes.

Not good.

Putting out of her head the millions of germs she'd likely come into contact with took some doing. If she didn't pay attention and ended up running into those men, germs would be the least of her worries.

Gibson moved into the adjoining corridor. She trailed after him, giving herself whiplash in an attempt to keep an eye on anything coming from any given direction. She wanted to ask where they were going, but risking conversation would be plain dumb. She remembered how easily they'd heard the others talking as they'd walked by that restroom. She didn't want to make the same mistake.

He hesitated at a door to one of the offices.

He withdrew a key from his pocket and let himself in. She moved in right behind him and carefully closed the door with the knob turned so the latch wouldn't make any noise sliding over the strike plate.

The office was pretty dark, but she would have recognized it if it had been pitch-black.

Gibson's office.

It smelled like him.

She drew in a deep breath, told herself it was for confirmation purposes.

"Did you come for your evidence?" she whispered as she edged up next to him.

"I'll get to that," he murmured back.

"Why are we in your office then?" Made sense to

her that they'd come here for the evidence he'd collected against his superiors.

"I want to see if this guy is in Welton's database."

"The one we left back in the restroom stall?"

Maybe that was a good idea, but she wasn't really sure what it would accomplish.

"Yeah." He leaned really close and it made her shiver. "You stay by the door and listen for trouble while I check it out. This may take a few minutes."

"Okay."

"You should sit to take the pressure off your injured leg."

Another good idea.

He helped her position a chair next to the door, then she settled into place to listen. The pain didn't subside entirely, but sitting definitely helped.

When he'd settled into the chair behind his desk she wondered exactly how he intended to check for the guy's name. The power was still off. The computer wouldn't be working, unless he had some sort of backup system she didn't have in her office.

He pulled a mass of papers from a desk drawer. No wonder he'd said it might take some time. There had to be fifty pages there. She watched as he took a small reading light, the battery-operated kind used for reading a book when traveling, from his desk. She wasn't worried about the light being noticed—there were no windows and the light was far too dim to reach beneath the door. As he flipped the first page she was even more distressed to see that names filled both the front and back of the pages. This would take all night.

While she waited for him to search the list of names, she thought about her work. She loved her job most of the time. Being good at that job was important to her. She tried not to think of tonight as any kind of failure on her part, though it clearly was on some level.

She should have had the foresight to call Mildred when the musicians didn't show on time. But she'd fallen asleep, ensuring she wasn't thinking straight when trouble first arrived. She should have hung onto the cell phone instead of dropping it when she stumbled onto Joseph's body. That was the dumbest thing she'd done tonight.

But then it was the first time she'd seen a murder victim.

Gibson worked furiously, his gaze sweeping the endless list of names. She wanted to ask him if he'd found anything yet, but she didn't want to risk missing any noise outside the door or making any of her own.

As she sat there, her leg throbbing and her shoulder sore, she wondered what her parents were doing. Her mom had tried to call her. Was she worried? They spoke every night at the same time. Would she wonder where her daughter was? They never discussed Elaine's social life. Maybe her mom knew without asking that her daughter rarely had a date and usually stayed at home with a book or a movie to keep her company. Steering clear of subjects that caused discomfort was an unspoken rule in her household.

Elaine glanced at the clock on the wall. Well past midnight. It was Christmas Eve.

Christmas Eve and she was still at the office… running for her life. She didn't even have a tree up. Not the first decoration.

She didn't care. Christmas wasn't such a big deal to her. Never had been. Why should she care if she didn't put up a tree?

Well, maybe she cared a little. It wasn't that she didn't like Christmas at all. It just…well, she despised the big deal everyone made of that particular holiday. The whole family and friends part seemed greatly overdone. She and her family had a nice quiet dinner, they didn't bother with gifts or caroling or any of that other stuff.

Elaine thought of the Christmas music that had awakened her at her desk tonight. Would that be the last holiday music she ever heard? Would her parents be dining alone this year? She definitely wouldn't have to worry about the Colby Agency Christmas party….

If she didn't make it out of this.

Her attention again shifted to the man behind his

desk. Would his family miss him when he didn't show for whatever Christmas plans they'd made?

What would really change if they both died tonight? Sure, their parents would be devastated for a while. Colleagues would discuss what a shame it was…but would anyone truly miss them? Maybe Gibson had friends like that, but she didn't…not really.

Her life was actually quite unremarkable. She worked. She went home. No one bothered her, she bothered no one. Really, what was there to miss?

For the first time in her entire life she wondered what it would be like to make a snowman or go from door to door caroling with a group of friends. She'd never done any of that. Her parents had always been too private…too conservative to behave so informally in public. Snow was for shoveling, not playing in. Private matters were best kept private.

She was twenty-six years old and she'd never done a single thing her parents wouldn't have approved of. Not once. Even her one intimate relationship in college had been with the blessing of her parents. They hadn't exactly given her permission to have sex, though she was sure they'd realized it was that kind of relationship, even if it hadn't lasted. It wasn't that she was such a perfect daughter or never made mistakes, she simply hadn't felt compelled to deviate from their rules, stated or implied. Their rules had become her rules with the same ease and predictability as her hair and eye color.

Well, okay, maybe running around the building with no stockings or shoes was one thing they would highly disapprove of, but that hadn't actually been a choice.

What was wrong with her?

Besides an injured leg and wrenched shoulder.

Why hadn't she let her hair down, figuratively speaking, long ago? She had this great job where lots of exciting people were about most any day of the week. There was an endless supply of intriguing clients, male as well as female. It wasn't as if she were an ugly cow or anything.

Then again, she didn't exactly get asked out on a regular basis. In fact, she couldn't recall the last time she'd been hit on by a guy, other than the video guy and he didn't count. She had decided he'd been bored that night.

Maybe it was the vibes she emitted. Or maybe guys simply weren't attracted to her. All the men she knew treated her like a little sister.

Her gaze settled on Brad Gibson. What did he see when he looked at her? There really hadn't been time to analyze what he did or didn't think. They were too busy avoiding being caught.

The pages of names were tossed aside, snapping her from the troubling thoughts.

His gaze collided with hers. Her cheeks burned at the idea that he'd caught her staring at him. "Did you…ah…" She cleared her throat. "Did you find anything?"

He shook his head and snapped off the reading light. "Nothing."

Good save. She gave herself a mental pat on the back.

She wondered if he'd really expected to find anything. Surely a firm as prestigious as Welton Investments wouldn't have any of their own people doing this kind of dirty work. Too easy to track back to them.

He pushed out of his chair with scarcely a creak and walked soundlessly over to where she waited by the door. She told herself not to watch his every sinuous move, but she couldn't resist. He crouched down in front of her.

"How're you holding up?"

She was pretty sure he meant her leg. "It hurts, but it's nothing I can't deal with."

"And your shoulder?"

He'd watched her fall. He had to know she'd wrenched the heck out of it grabbing onto the ladder to halt her downward plummet. The whole thing had been one tremendous lucky break for her.

She resisted the impulse to rotate her shoulder to prove it still worked. "Not as bad as it could be." That was the truth. She could be splattered all over one of those beams or, God forbid, all over the marble-floored lobby.

Oh, yeah, she'd been very lucky.

"I think it would be best," he said on the heels of a sigh, "if we found someplace safe for you to hide until this is over."

Was he crazy? He'd needed her in that restroom. That guy would likely have killed him if she hadn't helped out. She said as much, keeping her voice a whisper in spite of her irritation with his suggestion.

He scrubbed a hand over his face. She couldn't help measuring how he looked now against the way he'd looked when they first met tonight. His shirt was soiled and tattered, literally, and threads hung from the ragged edges where his sleeves once connected with the body of the garment. His hair was mussed and his eyes were weary. That was the part that bothered her most. He looked exhausted...resigned to defeat.

No way. She worked for the Colby Agency. Colby Agency personnel didn't admit defeat.

"We have to stick together, Gibson," she countered in a fierce whisper. "The only way we'll survive this night is if we come up with a plan and see it through. So don't go getting all down and out on me. I have things to do."

For the first time in her life she meant that last statement in the truest sense of the words. She'd let life pass her by long enough. It was time to live. Adrenaline soared, making her pulse kick into overdrive.

She was tired of being quiet Elaine who none of

the opposite sex really noticed unless it was to nudge her on the shoulder and make some inane, brotherly comment.

"Give up on your own time, Gibson," she snapped. She wasn't going to die a near virgin. Not that she was actually a virgin, but once hardly made her experienced.

She wanted to be experienced. In lots of things.

She wanted to be…something besides what she was.

"I wasn't planning on giving up," he assured, dragging her back to the here and now from that place she couldn't seem to stay away from—regret. "I just wanted to protect you from—"

"I can take care of myself."

That was another thing that got on her nerves. She'd been living on her own since graduating high school. To date she hadn't been mugged, ripped off or otherwise fooled by another human being. She kept a job, paid her bills on time and didn't have the first parking ticket on her record. She could damned sure take care of herself.

He stroked his chin, the sound of stubble making her feel quivery inside, but it was those steady gray eyes that made her feel as if she could do everything she hoped to do.

"I rescind the suggestion and offer my humblest apologies." The barest hint of amusement twinkled in his eyes.

"Apology accepted." She leaned forward, putting her face nose-to-nose with his. "So what's the plan, Gibson? We need a plan."

That his gaze dropped to her lips startled her, and also prompted another of those quivery sensations. Very exciting. She already liked this new, slightly more aggressive self. She liked even more that *she* had made this happen.

When he didn't answer immediately, she made a few suggestions of her own. "Shall we go for your evidence? Check out the fourth floor to see if there's anything going on in my agency? Or should we just stick with trying to escape with our hides intact?"

He sat back, putting some distance between them, but that analyzing gaze kept her in the crosshairs. "I'm going to need a minute to think about this."

She appreciated his prudence, but they already overstayed their welcome in the area as far as she was concerned.

As if to corroborate her concerns, the unmistakable sound of running footfalls echoed beyond the door.

The shouts that followed confirmed the worst.

They'd found the guy in the restroom.

"I don't think we have a minute, Gibson."

Chapter Eight

1:20 a.m.

"This way."

Brad ushered Elaine toward the far end of the corridor. If they were really fortunate they would make it around the next corner before all hell broke loose.

Only a few more yards.

At the point where the ninety-degree turn would take them in the direction they needed to go, Brad flattened against the wall and took a deep steadying breath before risking a glance around the corner. The silence bolstered his courage. He leaned around that corner....

Clear.

With Elaine's hand still clutched in his, he ran like hell toward the office of his colleague, Darren Turner. He'd hidden the files he needed in Darren's office for the same reason he was headed there now, to be somewhere the jerks on the other side of this very floor wouldn't think to look for him.

This floor had likely already been searched and deemed clear. He couldn't be sure what else they'd been doing in here, but checking each floor for their prey was pretty much a given. Since the bad guys now knew he and Elaine were, or had been, on this floor, they would have to assume he'd returned for something he'd left here. Which meant they would check his office first. There would be no reason for them to give Turner's office more than a cursory glance.

At least that was what Brad was banking on.

He slid the key into the lock, watchful of both ends of the corridor. Any second now those bastards could come flying around one of those corners.

He pushed the door inward, tugged Elaine inside with him and then locked the door. Good thing he'd had Turner's key duplicated. It hadn't been difficult. The guy was always leaving personal items lying around on his desk. Swiping the key one morning and then getting a copy made during his lunch break, he'd had it back on Turner's desk before he ever missed it. Brad told himself he hadn't done a bad thing. This evidence needed protecting, for the greater good.

Pushing the chair behind the desk out of the way, thankful it didn't squeak, he crouched down and reached under the middle drawer. His fingers went right to the jump drive he'd taped there. No larger than a Bic lighter, the storage stick held the key to his future. The key to justice. Not to mention a little revenge. These guys had tried to bury him. Now he'd have the pleasure of doing the burying.

"The files you needed?" Elaine didn't crouch down next to him. Probably because it would make the stitches pull and would hurt like hell.

"That's it." He thought about putting it into his pocket, but the risk of getting caught by these thugs was still too real. "I'm thinking this might be the safest place for it even now." Taping it back into place would more than likely be in his best interest.

Elaine chewed her lower lip a moment, evidently considering his theory. "You could be right." She flipped her hair over her shoulder. He watched her every move with far too much interest.

"Wait." This time she did ease down into a position somewhere between kneeling and crouching, but not without some reflection of the cost in her expression. "Why don't we put it into an in-house pouch and address it to Victoria, my boss. If we put it in the nearest mail drop…" A smile spread across her face. "They'd never in a million years think to look for it there and if…" She moistened those full lips. "If we don't make it through this, Victoria will see that justice is done."

He couldn't resist. He had to touch her. He

caressed her soft cheek with the pad of his thumb. God, she was beautiful. "You're a genius."

She blushed. He liked that about her. She was plenty sassy and gorgeous, but still sweet and very much down to earth.

"I'll write Victoria a note." She used the desk to lever herself back to her feet.

Brad located the necessary pouch while she wrote a fast and furious note to her employer. He placed the jump drive inside the eight-by-eleven nylon pouch, then held it open for her note.

She inserted the note into a clear plastic slot so that "The Colby Agency," written in her neat, bold strokes, was visible as the pouch's destination and then he zipped it closed.

Their gazes met and something resolute passed between them. No matter what happened tonight, the bad guys would get theirs. Victoria would trust her employee's assessment of the situation whether she had trusted Brad's or not. His name would be mud come tomorrow unless this evidence got into the right hands.

Now all he had to do was make it to the mail drop.

And convince Elaine to stay put.

He hitched a thumb toward the door. "I'm going to make a mail run." He tried to keep his tone light, teasing almost. They hadn't heard any noise from the enemy in a few minutes. Maybe they were lucky and they'd assumed he and Elaine had headed for another floor.

"I'm going with you."

This would be the hard part.

"You'll only slow me down." Before she could dispute his allegation he went on. "You stay here. Out of sight under the desk and I'll be right back."

It was a good plan.

All the way up to the moment when she opened her mouth to give him her reasons for doing the exact opposite. But she didn't get the chance to say a word.

They had company.

Not more than a few doors away.

He pointed to the desk.

She didn't argue.

For someone with an injured leg and a tender shoulder she was under that desk in three seconds flat. He wedged himself between the corner of the room and the end of the desk that was placed at an angle there. He had a bad feeling that getting out would be a lot harder than getting in.

The doorknob turned. He didn't have to see it. He heard the violent twist. He imagined that if these guys found him they would probably want to do something similar to his neck. Their patience was likely running thin. For a couple of civilians he and Elaine had given these guys a run for their money.

The metal on metal sound of a key inserting into

the lock echoed in the ten by twelve office. The subtle shift of the room's climate told him the door had opened even before he heard the first tread of a booted foot.

The beam of a high-powered flashlight moved around the room…hesitated on the desktop. For three thuds of his pulse, time seemed to stop. Then the light moved beyond the desk, over the filing cabinets.

The intruder moved out of the room, pulling the door shut behind him. The latch clicked into place. His steps faded as he moved to the other end of the corridor.

Brad closed his eyes and told himself he could keep doing this. He'd been gung ho to get started at the Colby Agency. The investigators surely found themselves in these positions quite frequently. He should consider this advance preparation. A pretraining drill.

If the Colby Agency still wanted anything to do with him after tomorrow.

For five long minutes Brad didn't move or speak. Elaine followed his example. He used the excuse that taking this much time was to ensure the enemy moved on to another floor, but it was, in part, because he was exhausted and he knew she had to be as well.

He wondered about her. Was she involved? Did she have plans for Christmas? Maybe, if they lived through this, he'd take her to dinner sometime. Just to show his gratitude for living through this with him. It had taken the both of them working together as a team to outwit these killers. Then again, they hadn't actually won the battle yet.

One step at a time, he reminded himself. They had to live through the next five minutes first.

When he felt confident no one was coming back that way, he wiggled out of the space he'd wedged himself into. Then he rounded the desk and gave Elaine a hand getting to her feet. The grimace she wore told him how much cramming herself under that desk had cost her.

He waited by the door, the pouch clutched in one hand. Get to the mail drop and then get the hell out of here. If the enemy had moved on as he suspected, it should be safe to venture out.

"I'm going for the mail drop," he murmured close to her hair. He liked the smell of her hair. Something sweet like berries. "I'll be back for you."

This time she didn't argue.

When he would have opened the door she tugged at his shirt. He turned back to her and couldn't miss the worry in her eyes.

"I really need you to come back for me, Gibson. Don't go out there and get yourself killed."

He liked that she was worried about him a lot more than he should have. "I'll be back."

With the same caution he'd used all night, he gradually opened the door. This was really getting old.

The corridor was clear.

He edged out of the office.

Now all he had to do was cover the next fifty or so yards without getting caught.

Straight down the corridor, one left turn and the mail drop was right there in the reception area.

No problem.

He started walking, measured steps designed to be noise free.

Almost there.

He pressed up against the wall at the corner. The reception area lay just around this bend.

No sound. No nothing.

Bracing for the worst, he swung around the corner.

Reception was empty.

He sprinted to the mail drop that sent letters and pouches down to the mail room in the basement of the building. His ability to breathe came a little easier once that pouch was on its way off the floor.

It wasn't until he'd turned around that he allowed his senses to absorb anything other than the presence of imminent threat.

Two elevator cars stopped on each floor in this building, not counting the freight elevator.

The brushed steel doors he'd stared at a thousand times while waiting for the car to arrive were partially open. The memory of the explosions they had heard just a couple of hours ago punched through the rest of his thoughts to claim a position front and center.

What the hell had they been blowing up?

Morbid curiosity drew him across the room…all the way to the brutalized doors. He shouldn't be hanging around out here, but he had to see.

He stared into the first shaft. Couldn't determine the reason for the explosions. Then he noticed the frayed metal that had once been tracks and observed that the cables that should have extended from the car stalled on the first floor all the way to the roof of the building were missing. He peered upward as well.

What was the point in destroying the elevator's cable system? He moved to the second set of doors. The same scenario. It didn't make sense. None of the events that had occurred tonight made sense. Once the enemy had forced the elevator doors open and verified that he and Elaine weren't hiding in the shafts, what was the point of doing additional damage? It wasn't as if they could use the elevators with the power out.

The hair on the back of his neck stood on end. Was it possible that this was about something other than him and the evidence he had against Welton Investments? He'd felt confident that wasn't the case, but he could no longer assume this was merely about his situation.

Maybe Elaine was right…this whole night could have been orchestrated by an enemy of the Colby Agency.

Only one way to find out.

Brad stole back to the office where he'd left Elaine. Keeping an eye on both ends of the corridor, he whispered just loud enough for her to hear him through the closed door, "Let's go."

She opened the door barely far enough to squeeze out. At her expectant look, he nodded a confirmation. "It's done."

Glancing first left then right, she grabbed his hand. "We should get out of here. They could come back."

The stairwell exit was on the side of the building opposite the lobby. Two simple turns. All they had to do was avoid any one of the killers who might still be searching for them on this floor. He hoped they'd all moved on already but he couldn't be certain.

At the second corner Brad got another of those bad feelings. Getting out of here would never be as simple as slipping into that stairwell.

Nothing about this night had been simple.

But he had to try.

Using Elaine's ring of keys, he attempted to open the door. Wouldn't budge. He tried again. The knob turned freely but the door wasn't moving.

"Let me try."

He stepped back and let her try her hand at it. Her luck was no better than his.

"They've done something. Blocked it from the other side or something." She rubbed at her forehead. She was tired.

"Maybe they've decided to try and pin us down to one floor." Sounded like the kind of plan these scumbags would come up with.

A distant rumble had them both turning back to look the way they'd come.

They heard the sound of clicking and metal sliding over metal accompanied by a deep hum.

Elaine's breath caught. "The freight elevator."

Before he could stop her, she headed in that direction.

"We need to avoid them," he whispered as he fell into step next to her, "not rush to meet them."

"I want to know where they're going." She glanced up at him. "And how that elevator is working with the power still out."

"What if their destination is here?"

"Then we'll head the other way."

Made perfect sense. Just like everything else happening around them.

At the corner where the corridor made a right and dead-ended at the freight elevator she hesitated.

Thank God. He'd worried that she would just barge right up to the elevator doors.

The grind of wheels and cables accompanied the elevator's upward movement.

It didn't stop on the second floor.

She moved around that corner and ran all the way to stand directly in front of it.

In the dead silence radiating around them the clink and scrape of the slow-moving car's ascent felt amplified a dozen times over.

"It stopped."

Though there was no readout displaying the floor numbers, she stared at the closed doors as if they'd somehow told her the car's final destination.

She turned her attention to him then. "Fourth floor. We have to get up there."

Somehow he'd known that would be her response.

"What's your plan?" Hadn't she asked him earlier what his plan was? She needed to think this move through before acting.

"I'll let you know when we get there."

Since he didn't really have a better idea and the night's events had just taken a definite turn for the mystifying, what the hell?

The stairwell was blocked. The elevators destroyed—except for the freight elevator, which the bad guys appeared to be using while leaving the rest of the building without electrical power. Not to mention it was noisy as hell.

That left the same overhead method they'd been utilizing.

Might as well go to a route they had used before.

He led the way back to the same restroom where they'd almost been caught. At least he knew what to expect above this room.

Upon initial inspection the restroom appeared clear of trouble. But once they'd gotten inside they saw what the killers had left behind.

Their friend.

The one Brad had hog-tied.

"Oh, God." Elaine turned away.

They hadn't bothered to untie him. The socks were still stuffed into his mouth. Apparently they hadn't bothered to question him, either. Just shot him twice in the head. Talk about rigid standards—screw up once and you're dead.

"Pretend he's not here," he suggested, not entirely convinced even he could do that. "We have to get off this floor and this is the way."

She nodded and moved cautiously into the stall where the dead man lay trussed up like a Thanksgiving turkey. She climbed up onto the toilet seat. Her feet were bare. Funny he'd just noticed those pink toenails. Cute.

He climbed up onto the toilet seat with her. When he'd steadied himself, working hard to ignore the feel of her body pressed against his, he reached up and pushed a ceiling tile out of place.

His hands wrapped around her waist. She was tiny. Felt soft. He could get used to touching her like this.

"Remember," she admonished.

"I know. No looking up your skirt."

He lifted her, kept his eyes shut tight as he'd

promised. When she'd hoisted herself up onto the beam, he pulled himself up to join her.

She wasn't going to like his suggestion.

"Not the ladder," she countered, reading his mind.

"Sorry, but it's the only way."

Resigned, she muttered, "Whatever."

She moved along the beams without any trouble. He'd been concerned about her leg, but she appeared to be holding up damned well. He hadn't noticed any seepage, which meant his handiwork was still holding.

The leftover parts of the emergency first-aid kit were tossed around the area where he'd conducted the rudimentary repair procedure. He didn't like looking at the reminder. Neither did she, it appeared. She strode straight over to the ladder and climbed on. He moved in behind her.

"I can do this, Gibson."

It was true. He knew it, but he thoroughly appreciated the feel of her body tucked against his. But the rest of the truth was that he didn't want to take any risks with her safety this time. They would be going even higher. He couldn't be sure her other fall had been caused by panic, but if she got nervous or distracted this time, the consequences would be devastating.

"I know you can. I just like being close to you."

She started upward. He stayed right behind her.

"Are you flirting with me, Mr. Gibson?"

He wasn't sure if it was hope he heard in her voice

or disbelief. "Do you want me to be flirting with you, Miss Younger?"

She hesitated before moving to the next rung and turned her head just far enough to give him a coy look. "Maybe."

The smile came of its own accord. Just another facet of this truly surprising night.

"Does this mean you don't have a girlfriend?"

He probably should have seen that one coming. But if the conversation kept her from getting nervous as they climbed upward, he was game. "No time for a girlfriend. How about you?"

"Just a couple."

A couple? He wasn't sure how he was supposed to respond to an answer like that. "You have two boyfriends?"

She laughed, the genuine article. It was the first time he'd heard her do that. He liked it.

"Girlfriends. A couple of girlfriends."

"Nice. But that doesn't tell me about your boy-friend."

A girl as pretty as her was bound to have at least one. Just his luck she'd be spoken for.

"No boyfriend."

He was the one missing a step this time.

This wasn't exactly the time to be that distracted.

"No time for dating?" he prodded.

"Haven't run into any boyfriend material lately."

He told himself not to feel insulted. He understood that she was talking about before tonight.

"The agency is having a Christmas party today. If we get through this, maybe you'd like to come."

He didn't burst her bubble by mentioning that with the elevators out of commission and the better part of the building a crime scene, the chances of anything going on in this building later today were slim to none.

"Is that an invitation to attend a social function with you, Miss Younger?"

They'd climbed four more steps before she answered. "Yes. It is."

A smile tugged at the corners of his mouth. "Saying no isn't an option since you may have to save my life before this night is over."

"Saying no isn't an option at all," she let him know. "And for the record, I've already saved your life once tonight."

Touché. "We may have to end up at this party with what we're wearing."

"In that case we might need to ditch the official party and have a private one of our own."

He wanted to pursue that line of thinking, but they'd just topped the fourth floor.

"This is where we get off."

"Lovely." She said the word carelessly and he'd heard the relief hovering behind the bravado.

She turned her attention from the ladder to the nearest beam.

He waited until she had moved a few feet away then he swung over to the beam. "That—" he pointed to the grid system of tiles near their feet "—is the ceiling over the reception area on your floor."

"Are we going down from here?"

"Someplace less public, I think."

The grind of the freight elevator moving once more had them staring off in that direction. Going down.

"We have to hurry, Gibson."

She was right.

"Give me the general layout of your floor. We'll pick a spot where they'll least likely be." He was familiar with reception and the corridor that led to Victoria's office, but that was it.

"I don't know...."

She appeared to struggle with the decision. He could hardly blame her. One wrong move and they could end up dead. Who wanted to be responsible for that?

"Wait." Inspiration cleared the worry from her face. "There's a restroom in the lounge."

Might as well stick with what worked. Restrooms appeared to be their ticket in and out around here tonight.

They made the precarious journey across the beams until they reached the small restroom located in the lounge.

Right away there was a problem.

"There's no dropped ceiling."

She stared at the back of the Sheetrock that had been used to form the ceiling of the room. The only way to go through there would be to kick a hole in the ceiling and that would make noise.

"We can either drop down into the lounge or select a new spot."

She considered that possibility then made a suggestion of her own. "Let's use the main supply room."

Another stellar idea.

A few minutes more were necessary for locating the supply room. He felt reasonably certain Elaine was tired and a bit disoriented. Things looked entirely different up here. She couldn't be expected to walk right to the room.

Once she'd located the supply room, they both listened to make sure they were alone in the vicinity.

The first ceiling tile he moved was for locating a storage cabinet or counter usable for a step. The next one was for escape. He helped Elaine down through the opening. When she'd managed to climb off the counter below, he took his turn.

The boxes and cabinets of supplies were meticulously organized. A wide counter, the one they'd used for a step, owned the center of the room. A large paper cutter sat on one end.

Brad moved to the door and listened. If the three

men left in this operation were on that elevator then the coast was clear for them to slip out of this room. But he needed to be sure.

She was already getting her key ready.

He held up a hand for her to wait. "We have to be sure there's no one waiting right outside this door."

She nodded her understanding.

Five minutes passed. No voices. No footfalls.

It sounded as if they were alone on the fourth floor.

"You ready?" She didn't look at him when she asked the question.

He wondered about that. "Yeah, I guess so."

He wasn't actually. Truth was he'd rather stay in here with her. Where they were safe...where they could talk about tomorrow.

But they couldn't do that.

They had a mission.

Find out what the hell was going on.

And stay alive.

Chapter Nine

1:45 a.m.

Elaine took a breath and opened the door.

She led this time. This was her territory.

Funny how that particular possessiveness came out in a time like this. She'd enjoyed working at the Colby Agency since day one. It was the sort of job one didn't dread going to, except maybe around holidays. But she hadn't realized this fierce determination to protect the agency existed deep inside her.

Doing a good job and risking one's life were two different matters. Still, she suffered no qualms about doing what had to be done.

The two large cases containing the bodies of the security guards still sat in the corridor near the freight elevator. An ache twisted in her chest when she thought of poor Joseph and the other man she hadn't known. This would be a horrible Christmas for their families. Their children would forever associate their deaths with this time of year.

They'd be more warped about the holiday season than she was. And that was sad.

Truly sad.

She turned in the opposite direction. If these killers were enemies of the Colby Agency then there were two places on this floor that they would consider primary target areas.

Victoria's office and the files room.

"Where're we headed?"

He'd spoken the question so softly she'd barely heard him above the guessing game playing out inside her head. She wished there were a way to contact Ian Michaels or Victoria Colby-Camp herself.

"Victoria's office."

If Gibson had any thoughts on how they should proceed he kept them to himself. She appreciated his confidence in her, though as she moved forward, drawing ever closer to her destination, uncertainty tugged at her.

Outside the wall of glass to her right, snow continued to fall. It had to be six or eight inches deep out there. The city looked beautiful with the lights glistening against the contrast of the dark night and the pure white snow.

She wished she were out there, building a snowman or just flopped onto her back flapping her arms and legs to form a snow angel. She'd never done the former and couldn't actually recall making the latter. Why couldn't she have been a little more like everyone else? Why had her parents been so untouchable on so many levels?

More important, why had she turned out just like them?

Elaine pushed the thoughts away. She loved her parents and right now she had far more to worry about than making snow angels.

Mildred's office had been ransacked. The sight drew her up short. The feel of Gibson's comforting hand at her back made the realization easier to take.

This had to be about the Colby Agency.

Two people had died already and no one capable of saving the day had any idea.

She felt bad for thinking that. Gibson had done a great job of saving the day so far. She'd even helped a little. Maybe guys like Ian Michaels and Simon Ruhl could have done more, but it was the effort that counted.

Careful of the wreckage on the floor, she made her way to Victoria's door. It stood open.

Elaine stalled there, taking in the ruins for several seconds before she could move into the room.

If Mildred's office was ransacked, Victoria's was destroyed beyond recognition.

Every piece of furniture, even the curtains, were ripped and shredded and shattered.

Victoria had used this office for more than twenty years and now it was nothing more than scattered fragments of that distinguished history.

Elaine started into the room, but Gibson held her back.

"Too much broken glass," he pointed out.

She glanced down at her feet. He was right. She couldn't remember what she'd done with her boots. She'd left them somewhere, in the restroom in the lobby maybe. She definitely didn't need an injured foot.

"There's nothing we can do here."

She turned to him. "We need to get to the files room. That's most likely where whatever they're looking for is kept."

Elaine retraced her path to the room they'd already passed. She didn't know why she hadn't stopped there first, maybe because she'd somehow realized that Victoria's office stood for all that the agency represented, making it a prime target in the event this act was motivated by vengeance.

She'd been right to think that.

The files room door was closed, as were all the other doors along that corridor. She located the proper key and unlocked the door.

As she entered she didn't know why she was surprised, but somehow she was.

The ten flat-panel computer monitors had been smashed. Dozens of filing cabinet drawers hung open. A couple of cabinets lay face down on the floor, their contents spewed all around. But the most frightening element of the destruction she noticed was the missing CPU towers. Every single one had been taken, whatever data saved there now a hostage in the enemy's hands.

Elaine turned all the way around in the room, the need to do something, to act on the adrenaline flowing through her, making her heart pound furiously.

"I have to get word to Victoria."

She would be devastated.

The radio tucked into Gibson's back pocket suddenly crackled to life.

Elaine jumped. She'd forgotten about the radio they'd taken off the guard.

Gibson ripped the radio out of his pocket and held it close to his ear.

"Eighth floor is prepped."

The voice was muffled, but the words were plenty distinct.

Elaine wanted to ask "Prepped for what?" but she stayed very still and very quiet in the event one of the killers said more.

"Help Bauer with six."

It seemed odd to her that these men had maintained radio silence since she and Gibson lifted the radio. Suddenly now they're talking. Either the guys were stupid or they were attempting to confuse her and Gibson.

"We should move."

Apparently Gibson had the same thought.

She'd taken only one step toward the door when it burst inward.

An intense beam of light hit her right in the face. Gibson had a spotlight as well. She lifted her hand in front of her face to shield her eyes.

"Drop the weapon and the radio."

That was another thing she'd forgotten. Gibson had the dead man's gun.

"If I don't?"

Elaine tensed, hoped like hell Gibson wasn't about to get himself killed.

"If you don't *she* dies."

So it wasn't his life he'd just risked.

He placed the gun on the floor and toed it toward the bad guys, then did the same with the radio and extra ammunition clip. A sinking feeling sucked at her stomach. They were doomed for sure.

"Who are you?"

Elaine was startled to realize the words had come from her.

"An old friend of your employer."

That answer told her nothing at all. But considering three weapons were trained on the two of them, she had no intention of pointing that out.

"I'm sure Victoria will be sorry she missed you."

That remark didn't garner so much as a smirk from their captors. Not that she could actually tell since the three were wearing masks, but judging by their grim mouths, which she could see plainly, and the hard look in their eyes, they didn't get the joke.

"We need your user name and entry code for the electronic files."

Elaine heard the request, but it didn't actually penetrate as it should have right away. She was too busy considering the idea that she wasn't nearly as frightened as she should be. Had the fact that she'd seen a friend, Joseph, lying murdered on the floor somehow desensitized her? Or maybe it was the whole running-for-her-life thing the past few hours. Or the near-fatal fall from that damned ladder. Whatever the reason, she felt kind of numb.

The man who'd asked her the question jerked his head toward her and the man to his left stepped forward.

Uh-oh.

Fear fired through her veins making the soles of her feet and her fingertips burn.

Gibson stepped in front of her. "She's a reception-ist, she doesn't have the information you want."

The minion who'd come after her elbowed Gibson in the stomach, then whacked him on the head with the butt of his weapon.

Elaine pressed her fingers to her mouth to hold

back a scream. She didn't know why she bothered to stifle the sound, maybe habit from keeping quiet since this thing started.

She tried to rush to where Gibson lay crumpled on the floor but the man stopped her. Gibson stirred, then dragged himself to a sitting position. Thank God.

"Give me your user name and password," the man in charge demanded.

She faced him, wished she had a weapon. "Don't you have someone who can break into the system? Surely anyone who could put together an operation this large would have other assets besides brawn."

This time she got the elbow to the gut.

The wind whooshed out of her lungs and the gag reflex was instinctive. At least she didn't throw up.

"I'll ask you once more—what is your user name and password?"

Sticking with what Gibson said, she answered, "I don't have one."

The man in charge shifted his attention to the elbow guy. "Kill him."

Terror wrapped bony fingers around her throat. Before she could force her voice beyond that constriction the elbow fiend had drawn his weapon and aimed it at Gibson.

"EYounger twenty-six!" The information burst from her throat. "Lonelygirl."

Ben was going to kill her. Ben Haygood was the

resident computer guru at the agency. He'd ensured that the electronic security was impenetrable. He would really be disappointed in her for letting the whole agency down.

But she couldn't let these thugs kill Gibson.

She'd done the right thing.

"Very good, Elaine."

She shuddered at the way he said her name.

He turned to the man who'd drawn his weapon on Gibson and said, "You know what to do with him."

A new lash of terror assaulted her. "Wait! I gave you the information you wanted."

"Yes, you did. And that's the only reason you're going to survive this night, Elaine. It's my gift to you. An early Christmas present."

"Please don't do this!" She stood there helpless as Gibson was shoved toward the door. She couldn't let this happen. This was wrong...wrong...wrong. Gibson didn't have anything to do with this. She was the one who worked for the Colby Agency. "Take me instead."

Those three words rang for what felt like minutes. Every man in the room stopped and stared at her.

She moistened her trembling lips and pushed on. "He doesn't work for the Colby Agency. He has nothing to do with this. Take me. Let him go." She swallowed back the lump of cold, hard fear rising in her throat. "Give him the Christmas present."

"Well, well, we have ourselves a martyr here."

"Don't listen to her," Gibson said. "She's lying. I work for the Colby Agency the same as she does. Only I'm an investigator. So whatever you've got in mind, you can do it to me."

What the hell was he saying? "Gibson, you're—"

"Don't say anything else, Elaine," he snapped.

The guy with the restless elbows slammed Gibson in the abdomen again.

"This is just too sweet for me," the man in charge sneered. "Take him," he barked at his comrade.

Elaine's knees shook, but she forced herself to remain steady. She wanted to say more, to tell Gibson she was sorry, but emotion had tied her tongue in knots.

His gaze held hers one last moment before his captor shoved him out the door. No, no, this wasn't right.

The door slammed shut, leaving her with these two men with their masks and their guns.

She'd taken so much for granted…like her time with Gibson. She hadn't told him how much she appreciated the way he'd helped her. How much she'd enjoyed spending time, even running for their lives, with him.

"As soon as my colleague has confirmed the user name and password you provided, we'll almost be finished here."

"Who are you?" she had to ask.

He laughed, long and loud. "You don't really expect me to tell you who we represent, do you?"

She shivered as his cruel voice raked across her senses. This man really was evil. "Why did you have to kill the security guards? It's Christmas, for God's sake. How do you think their children are going to feel?"

What the hell was wrong with her? This guy didn't care about anyone, much less Christmas. He'd only been toying with her when he'd said she would survive this night as a Christmas gift. She should just keep her mouth shut. But she couldn't. She had to do something…had to try.

Gibson was depending on her, whether he knew it or not.

"The security guards are dead because they went for their weapons. Overreacting can be hazardous to your health."

Bastard. What had he expected them to do when confronted with armed men?

"They'll be hauled to the maintenance level just like your friend."

Maintenance level. That was in the basement along with the mail room and long-term storage.

The security guards were in those equipment cases….

"What did you do with those musicians?" She hated this man. She didn't even know his name but she hated him.

"Let's just say they're enjoying the snow."

God, he'd killed them, too. But then she'd known they were probably dead.

She couldn't just stand here. She had to do something.

Maybe keep him talking until she could think of a plan.

"What are you doing with the freight elevator?" Other than moving those cases with the bodies in them, she didn't bother adding.

"Moving files and equipment. Who wants to use the stairs with their arms full?"

They'd been carrying down the computer towers and the files. Another wave of dread washed over her. This was going to be devastating to the Colby Agency.

The worst was that the sanctity of the client privilege would be breached. All that information in the hands of an enemy.

Focus, Elaine. Keep him talking. Learn all you can.

"Why does the freight elevator work when there's no power?" Good. Something else he'll want to brag about. He won't be able to resist championing his skill.

"We're in control of the whole building, Elaine." He pulled what looked like a bulky remote control from inside his jacket. "I can dim lights, brighten them, allow the power to only one office or a whole floor, and, of course, operate any or all elevators."

No wonder the silent alarm hadn't activated and

nothing seemed to work right. This guy had every-thing just like he wanted it. He'd been playing games with them all night.

She wanted to hurt him. "How long does it take your friend to confirm whether or not he can access the system? I could have done it a hundred times already."

"Why the hurry, Elaine? Can't wait to see if I deliver on that Christmas gift?"

This would probably be her last one.

The thought came out of nowhere and shook her to the very core of her being.

She was only twenty-six. Gibson probably wasn't much older. And they were both going to die because some jerk wanted his revenge.

But Gibson didn't deserve what was happening to him.

"I need to go to the bathroom." She crossed her legs for effect.

"We'll be leaving soon, Elaine. Trying anything rash will only lessen your likelihood of surviving."

She produced an annoyed glower for him. "This is about having to pee, not about your stupid agenda."

He glanced at his remaining comrade. "Take her, I'll finish up here. We'll rendezvous at the elevator."

Elaine allowed the other man to drag her into the corridor. She pretended resignation to her plight. When they reached the ladies' room door he shoved her against it and then followed her inside.

This wouldn't work with him in here. Might not work at all. But she had to try.

"No way am I going to do my business with you in here." She braced her hands on her hips. "I need privacy."

He shook his head. "No way."

She threw her hands up in the air. "Where am I going? There's only one way in or out."

He glanced around the restroom, weighing the idea.

"Will you please hurry?"

"I'll be right outside the door."

She pushed her lips into a feigned smile. "Thank you."

When he'd stepped outside the door, she rushed to the last stall and considered whether or not she could actually do this. She didn't know but she had to try.

Pain arced up her thigh as she climbed up onto the toilet lid. Thank God the women's toilets had lids. She couldn't reach the ceiling from there as Gibson had, but she could climb a bit farther up and do it. She braced her right foot on the pipe that thrust upward at the back of the commode and grabbed onto the side wall of the stall. When she'd propelled herself up onto one foot, she reached for a ceiling tile with her free hand. Her shoulder hurt like hell, but she had no choice but to use both arms.

She got the tile scooted out of the way. Relief

gushed through her when she saw the steel beam running parallel to the opening. Exactly what she needed.

Using all her strength and a whole lot of adrenaline, she grabbed onto the beam with one hand, then the other. For two or three seconds she was sure she would fall. She could barely hang on and her shoulder stung so badly it brought tears to her eyes.

She pulled herself upward, thrust her uninjured leg up into the ceiling and wrapped it around the beam. Now, all she had to do was lever her body the rest of the way up. It wasn't easy but she managed. Before moving, she slid the ceiling tile back into place. Then she took off, rushing along the beam as if she'd done this a million times.

Thankfully they hadn't questioned their friend before killing him or he would have told them that she and Gibson had been using this route.

Too bad for them.

She had to get to the basement. That's where they'd taken Gibson.

That meant only one thing to Elaine.

She'd have to go down that ladder.

Chapter Ten

2:20 a.m.
The home of Lucas and Victoria Colby-Camp

The telephone rang.

Victoria roused from troubled sleep.

Lucas lifted his head from his pillow. "I'll get it."

She patted her husband's shoulder. "That's all right, I'll get it. It may be Jim."

"It might very well be for me," Lucas warned.

That she didn't doubt, but she hadn't been sleeping well anyway. The idea that the baby could come any time now had her on edge. She dismissed the other feelings of anxiety she'd suffered earlier and reached for the extension on the bedside table.

"Hello."

"It's time."

Victoria's heart lifted. "It's time?"

"Tasha and I are on our way to the hospital now. I've already called Dr. Rice."

Anticipation rushed through Victoria. "We'll be right there. Drive safely, Jim."

She hung up the receiver and breathed her first sigh of relief in several months. She sent a silent prayer heavenward giving thanks for the baby's safe journey thus far and asking for that blessing to continue.

"It's time, Lucas." She switched on the bedside lamp and turned to her husband.

She was certain the smile on her lips matched that of her husband's. They had both looked forward to this moment with such eager anticipation.

"I heard." Lucas threw back the down-filled covers. "We should get ready then."

Victoria jumped to her feet. "You're right. I don't know what I'm waiting for."

Lucas's smile widened to a grin. "It's the excitement, that's all. The baby is about to arrive and Christmas is upon us." He came around to Victoria's side of the bed. "This holiday belongs to you, my dear. Your every wish is about to come true."

Victoria's nerves jangled. He was right. This was the pinnacle she'd waited for for so very long. Complete happiness not only for herself, but for her son. After all he'd suffered in his life he deserved it so very much.

What was she doing standing around here reflecting on the past? She had to get dressed and plow her way through the snow to get to that hospital.

Thank God for four-wheel-drive SUVs and fearless husbands.

One hour later Victoria and Lucas were waiting in the lobby designated for the families of patients about to give birth. Strangely enough only two other families waited. According to the desk nurse dozens of families had come and gone during the course of the night. Things had slowed and the nursing staff appeared to be glad.

Lucas chatted with another grandfather-to-be. Victoria felt a familiar smile spread across her lips once more. Her husband was so handsome. She was so blessed to be able to share this moment with him.

An instant of regret trickled inside her at the reality that James Colby was not here to see his grandchild born. He would have been such a good grandfather. But she knew her first husband as well as she knew herself. Since he could not be here himself, he would want Lucas here. They had been the closest of friends. Closer than brothers.

James would not have resented in any way Lucas's place in this family.

Victoria smoothed a hand over her dress. It was foolish, she knew, but she'd wanted something special to wear when her grandchild arrived. She'd bought this dress just for this occasion. A deep royal blue sheath that made her feel young and vibrant. She'd thought about finally getting the multiplying silver among her ebony strands colored, but she'd decided against it. She didn't mind her age. She had far too many precious memories to regret a single moment of the time she'd spent on earth.

There was pain in her history, that was true. But every moment of every day had brought her to this place where the man she loved stood beside her and the son she adored had all that he should. And there was the Colby Agency. The agency thrived, held a very special place in her heart.

As soon as Jim brought the news of the baby's safe arrival and whether a granddaughter or a grandson, she would start making calls. The entire staff had insisted on being informed regardless of the hour. A roster of who would call whom had been arranged months ago. Victoria was to call Mildred and Ian, who would in turn call two others and so on until everyone had received the news.

Lucas moved to her side and took her hand. "Would you like me to make a fresh pot of coffee?"

Coffee sounded wonderful but the partial pot on the burner smelled as if it had been there a while.

"That would be much appreciated, Lucas." She pressed a hand to her chest and admitted, "If I tried right now I'd likely break something."

He squeezed her hand. "I could use a cup myself."

Her charismatic husband charmed the others in the room as he made a show of preparing a fresh pot. Everyone was nervous and needed a distraction. Lucas kindly provided that distraction. No one in the room would ever suspect that he was also a master spy. No one in the intelligence world was closer to the president himself.

That was Lucas. A man like no other.

A second pot of coffee had been brewed by the time Jim made an appearance at the door.

The undeniable happiness in those blue eyes spoke volumes. "They're bringing Tasha to a room now. Hurry." He motioned for her and Lucas to follow him. "Come and see your granddaughter."

Victoria's heart filled to bursting with joy. "A girl?"

Lucas patted his pockets. "And I forgot my cigars."

Victoria arrowed him a look. "No cigars." Then she hugged her son. "Congratulations, Jim."

He hugged her tightly, something he'd only begun to do a few short months ago. "I can't believe it," he murmured in her ear.

When they'd pulled apart Lucas offered his hand. "Congratulations, Jim, your father would be very proud."

Jim pumped Lucas's hand firmly. "He would be proud of a lot of things."

Victoria knew her son meant Lucas and how happy he'd made her.

"Let's go, boys." She ushered the men forward. "That child is waiting. And so am I."

Jim led the way to the private room. He kissed his wife, who looked absolutely beautiful despite having just given birth. Tasha and Victoria hugged. Tears were shed. There was no accounting for social formalities during a time like this.

Then the moment arrived—a nurse came into the room with the baby. A white receiving blanket covered in pink bunnies swaddled the beautiful little girl.

Tasha held her first, then Jim.

Finally Victoria had the child in her arms. Her color was gorgeous, her little chubby cheeks perfect. All was exactly as it should be down to ten tiny toes.

"We're going to name her Jamie." Tasha touched her baby's forehead. "Jamie Colby."

Victoria had promised herself she wouldn't cry again but that assurance wasn't holding up.

"That's lovely." She smiled down at her granddaughter. "Jamie. I like that."

Everything was perfect. Victoria was certain nothing would ever top this momentous occasion.

And still…something felt wrong. That uneasiness that had started before midnight hadn't let go. She'd fooled herself into thinking all was as it should be once Lucas had made it home.

But that wasn't true. She'd slept fitfully. She'd kept waking up and sensing some imminent doom.

Something very bad was about to happen and she couldn't fathom what it could be.

Chapter Eleven

2:16 a.m.
Inside the Colby Agency

Brad couldn't remember ever feeling this much pain.

But the pain was good. At least he knew he was alive.

For a while there he'd thought that might not be the case, but the guy who'd been using him as a human punching bag had apparently gotten bored and went off to do some other important work.

Lucky for him.

He tried to sit up, but a fire ripped through his ribs so he collapsed back against the concrete floor. He craned his neck in an attempt to see if his steroid-pumped friend was still around.

He couldn't see much for all the electrical and plumbing works. Large, standing tool boxes and a lot of warning signs on doors. This was one part of the building he could safely say he'd never seen before.

But it was the heart of the building in more ways than he'd known. This was where the power came from…when it was working, of course.

The emergency lights did little more than give the area an eerie feel, kind of like a technological grave-yard. Smelled like a machine shop, like hot metal and grease.

His mind was rambling, a pathetic attempt at dis-tracting him from the pain.

He had to stop that. He needed to find a way to get loose and help Elaine. Fear twisted in his chest whenever he thought of what they might have done to her.

When he'd been threatened she'd immediately jumped to his rescue, even offering to take his place. The act of courage stunned him even now.

How many people would do that? Especially for someone she'd known only a few hours.

He had to get back to her…had to rescue her.

Fury fed his adrenaline and he struggled to sit up once more. They'd tied his hands behind his back and his feet to a vertical metal support beam. His hands were all but locked together, allowing for only marginal movement. The bindings were tight, but if he kept at it he might be able to work them loose enough to slip his hands free.

The thin ropes cut into his skin but he didn't care. He had to get loose. Blood bloomed and trickled from his wrists, but that was good. The blood would help him work the ropes down and over his hands.

Focus on the goal, ignore the pain.

He struggled with all the energy he could rally. Gritted his teeth to hold back the groans of discomfort that automatically welled in his throat. Harder and harder he fought against the ropes.

Dammit.

This just wasn't working fast enough.

He needed a way to create a more intense friction against the ropes. A way to wear through and weaken the material restraining him.

But it wasn't like he could move.

He surveyed his position again, looked for anything that would help create the necessary friction.

Nothing was close enough for him to reach.

Except the steel beam.

Considering his position, there was only one way to attempt this. He rolled onto his stomach, suffered three kinds of hell most likely related to one or more fractured ribs. Using his chin and hunched shoulders, he propelled himself up onto his knees.

He was getting there.

Sucking in a ragged breath, he braced for the next hurdle: hefting himself to his feet, which would force his back against the steel beam.

It could work.

He gave it his best shot, lost his balance and

slammed back down onto the concrete floor face first. The breath burst from his lungs. Pain exploded in his abdomen.

As soon as the discomfort had minimized to a tolerable level, he tried again.

This time he pushed hard enough to make full contact with the beam. He swayed once, but then flattened against the metal surface.

A minute was required to get the nausea under control and then he was ready. Feverishly he rubbed his bindings against the edge of the post. He had to work harder, faster, break down the material. He closed his eyes and pictured the first layer giving way. The pain was irrelevant. He had to focus on breaking down one layer at a time.

The grip of the ropes on his wrists lessened a fraction. A fresh shot of adrenaline boosted his efforts. He poured every ounce of energy he had left into the struggle.

Another layer split.

He jerked his hands apart as far as possible. Yanked again and again until the bindings started to fall loose. One last twist and he was free. The abrupt release sent him off balance and he barely caught himself quickly enough to land on his knees rather than his face.

He shifted to a sitting position and worked at the restraints around his ankles. Blood dripped down his fingers as he dragged off his shoes and socks. He used the blood to lubricate the skin around the bindings, then tugged repeatedly until he was able to slip free one foot at a time.

Stepping back into his shoes, he scanned the area to be sure no one had come in while he was preoccupied.

Nothing. No sound. Not even rattling pipes since the power had been off for hours now. He shivered, realizing just how cold he was for the first time.

Elaine.

He had to find her.

Moving as quickly as the pain would allow, he weaved through the barrage of pipes and free-standing mini power stations. He couldn't remember exactly where the entrance was. He'd been too busy struggling with his captors.

He finally spotted the exit sign over the door. If he hadn't been so exhausted he might have noticed it sooner and not lost precious seconds.

But this wasn't the right door. It appeared to be an exterior door. If he could get this door open they could escape. It was worth a try.

He body slammed the door a few times, fought with the knob. Nothing worked.

The door wasn't budging short of using a crowbar and sledgehammer, all of which would make entirely too much noise and might very well set off an alarm, warning the enemy of their location. Even opening the door might set off an alarm. And all that was moot without the crowbar and sledgehammer.

He had to find Elaine first. Any escape attempts he made might put her in further jeopardy. If the worst hadn't already happened.

He refused to believe that. If they hadn't killed him, why would they kill her? He'd heard the man who appeared to be in charge say that he intended to let her live…as a Christmas present. What a freak.

He wandered aimlessly for a couple more minutes before he got his bearings and found the door he was looking for. His shoulder landed a little harder than he'd intended against the doorframe and he listened for any sound beyond the door. Nothing. But could he trust his senses at this point? The pain and adrenaline had the blood charging through his body, roaring in his ears and threatening his equilibrium.

When he started to reach for the doorknob, a sound, maybe a footstep, in the corridor beyond the door made him hesitate. He listened again. Didn't hear anything. Had he only imagined the sound?

The knob on the door twisted.

The urge to run raced along his lower limbs. Was the door locked like all the other interior doors? He tried to remember if the men who'd brought him down here had hesitated at the door long enough to have unlocked it before dragging him through it.

He slid behind the nearest cluster of electrical panel boxes and watched as the door eased open a crack.

If he stayed perfectly still and absolutely quiet they would think he'd already made a run for it. Once they were gone he would do just that.

The door opened wider and Elaine ventured cautiously inside.

She was alone.

Going weak with relief, Brad whispered her name.

Her head jerked left.

He slipped out of hiding and joined her at the door. "Are you all right?"

She surveyed him from head to toe and back. "The better question is, are you?"

He wanted to hug her. To tell her he was fine now, but there wasn't time. "They could come back any minute." He wished he'd thought of that when he'd been wasting time trying to open that door.

She took his hand, her eyes relaying the urgency even before she spoke. "We have to hide. We won't be able to use our usual route."

"I discovered what might be an exit down here." He looked back toward the other door. He couldn't see it from where he stood, but he knew it was there. Was he suffering from hallucinations?

"Before we waste any time and risk being caught again, we should take a few minutes to regroup and see how these guys are going to react to our escape."

What she said made sense, even if he was too tired to appreciate the thoughtful analysis.

Once out the maintenance door, she led him through the basement corridor. The pipes snaking overhead and the ambience of being deep below the ground when he was certain it wasn't more than a dozen or so feet beneath the snow-covered grass added another layer of uneasiness.

He wanted to ask her what she had in mind, but any noise was too much risk. No carpeting or elegant furnishings to absorb the sound. The slightest sound would carry much farther down here, bouncing off the cold uncluttered walls and bare floors. The fiery pain howled through him, diverting his focus when he couldn't afford to be distracted.

She didn't slow until they'd reached the stairwell door. She hesitated then and tiptoed so she could whisper close to his face. "We're heading for the lobby."

He wanted to frown but his face hurt too badly. He imagined both eyes were swelling fast as was the left corner of his mouth. "Why the lobby?" There had to be a better plan of action. He just couldn't think of one right now. Thinking at all was hard work, otherwise he would have already asked more about her plan.

She took another of those seconds of which they were in such short supply and seemed to gather her courage. "We're going to hide in plain sight."

He was too weary to argue and managed a nod.

Using a key from the ring of keys she wore on her wrist, once more she unlocked the stairwell door and eased it inward. He wondered briefly why they hadn't taken the keys when they had the chance. He'd had them last, hadn't he? Maybe he'd dropped them in the files room...he couldn't remember. Probably hadn't expected her to get away. They had the same keys, but taking hers would have limited her mobility. Maybe they liked allowing the thread of hope, giving them just enough confidence to keep trying to get away.

"We're good." She pulled him into the stairwell, then let the door close silently behind them.

Her leg hurt. She didn't have to say so, he read the pain on her face.

When they'd reached the exit to the first-floor lobby, she ensured the coast was clear before they emerged into the open.

She stayed close to the wall, urging him along after her with the tug of her small hand. He liked the feel of her hand in his. This wasn't exactly the time to be dwelling on something so irrelevant to their survival, but it beat the hell out of letting the pain carry his full attention.

When she reached the end of the corridor, she pressed close to him. "We need to move across the lobby to the snack shop. We can hide there."

"Won't it be locked?" He was reasonably certain that was the one fatal error in her plan.

"We can hide behind the tables. I did it before. They won't expect us to hide out in the open like this." She squeezed his hand. "Trust me, Gibson. It's about the only option we have left."

"Could work." He wished he'd been able to marshal a little more enthusiasm, but he was lucky to be standing at this point.

She nodded. "Let's make a run for it then."

The security desk sat in the center of the lobby, deserted and somber without Joseph waiting behind it to clear the comings and goings of the many clients and employees who entered the premises each day.

All they had to do was make it to the other side of that wide expanse of open territory and duck into the side corridor that led past the newsstands and straight to the snack shop.

Sounded simple enough.

A thought occurred to him and he decided to run it by Elaine and see what she thought. "Should we make a stop at the security desk and check the monitors to see if we can locate those guys?" As far as he could tell the security monitors and the emergency lights were the only electrical components still operational. Too bad the phones weren't a part of that glitch. Oh, yeah, and somehow the freight elevator worked.

"Good idea."

Another visual sweep of the lobby and they were off. He found himself watching her bare feet as she rushed to the halfway point—the security desk. Her feet were small, like her, and joined delicate ankles that led into toned legs. As his gaze reached the hem of her skirt he thought of those sassy pink panties again.

His brain had obviously turned to mush. Just now very little else about him was soft.

They dropped down behind the security desk, their gazes fixed on the monitors.

One man was moving down a corridor on the fifth floor. The screen identified the floor. As they watched, he unlocked and entered one of the offices.

"What's he doing?"

Brad shook his head. "Don't know. That's Stable Life Insurance, lots of branch offices all over the country."

As they watched, the man exited the office and moved on to the next one on the interior side of the corridor. It was then that Brad noticed the knapsack he carried. Evidently Elaine picked up on it at the same time.

She pointed to the screen. "What's in the bag?"

"Don't know."

"We need to know where the others are."

He caught movement in his peripheral vision on another monitor. Another masked man exited the files room on the fourth floor. He carried more Colby Agency files. The files were tucked under his arm, openly, as if he didn't care who saw him.

"Where's the third guy?" She shifted next to him. "He's probably looking for me right now. They may not realize you've escaped just yet."

Brad felt a frown taking hold of his features, setting off a new bombardment of pain.

Why wasn't the second floor showing up on any of the monitors?

He studied each one as it ran through its cycle, moving from corridor to corridor, floor to floor and sweeping the reception area of each level.

Except the second floor.

"Is this security footage recorded?"

"You're asking me?"

He hadn't actually meant to say the words aloud. A theory had started to take shape. If the feed was recorded then why the hell weren't these guys more worried about all that was being captured? Sure they wore masks, but even masked criminals were occasionally ID'd by body language.

And what had happened to the cameras on the second floor?

A malfunction? The emergency lights hadn't been

working properly there as he recalled. Some burning, others not.

The stairwell exits had been barricaded as well.

Just when he'd been certain this might very well be about the Colby Agency he noticed something about the ongoing drama that appeared to indicate otherwise. Pointed to Welton Investments.

No, they were here for the Colby Agency. That was why the bastard in charge had demanded Elaine's user name and password. No one had asked him anything about Welton Investments.

With the electrical system shutdown, any number of malfunctions could have occurred. The lights and cameras going out on one floor could have been coincidence. The barricaded stairwells, well, he didn't have an explanation for that part.

"Shall we make a run for the snack shop?" If he sat here too long he would only get stiff and have trouble moving. This location definitely wasn't a good hiding place. The enemy could just as well come by to check the monitors. And he didn't want Elaine out in the open any longer than necessary.

"I don't think I've ever wanted to see that snack shop more than I do right this minute."

Moving into position on one knee, he prepared to launch himself into a standing position and make a run across the rest of the lobby to the corridor that led to the snack shop. He'd let her lead the way since she'd done this before.

Elaine shifted into a crouch, her fingers touching the floor on either side to steady herself.

They both listened for several seconds.

Silence.

She made the first move, propelling herself into a run that favored her left leg.

Brad was right behind her.

She scrambled under a table that sat close to the shop's glass front. He ducked down and settled in next to her.

No wonder she'd said they would hide in plain sight—it was fairly open. But then the other tables and chairs placed around the small eating area provided a sort of camouflage. This could work.

The rasp of a rubber sole against cold marble ricocheted in the air, whispered against his eardrum.

Maybe they were about to face the first test of their hiding place.

The masked man, his black combat attire, boots included, giving him the look of a SWAT team member, moved warily around the lobby. His weapon palmed and ready for use, he checked the security desk as if he sensed they had only recently been there.

Brad felt Elaine tense next to him. He wished he could offer some sort of reassurances, but the best he could do was stay as still as possible, as quiet as possible, and hope for the best.

It wasn't until the guy started in their direction that Brad's tension ratcheted up several notches.

The man moved with that same deliberate caution, his gaze panning the one-eighty zone around him.

The closer he came to the tables, the more Brad was convinced their camouflage wouldn't cut it. The impulse to make a move was nearly irresistible. It felt wrong to sit here while the enemy came closer and closer knowing that he could spot them at any second.

A crackle from the man's radio shattered the tension-fraught silence.

He slid the radio off his utility belt, his gaze constantly panning the area. "Yeah."

"Need you on the fourth floor."

"On my way."

The man executed an about-face and strode back across the lobby.

The relief Brad felt was so intensely profound that it literally hurt. A shuddering exhale next to him reminded him that he wasn't the only one who'd suffered extreme tension just then. The idea that this was not the first time they'd been so lucky wasn't lost on him.

"They're destroying the agency one piece at a time."

Brad shifted his gaze to the woman next to him.

He sensed how torn she felt. She wanted to do something to stop the travesty taking place, but they were helpless to do anything more than protect themselves.

"We can't stop them, Elaine."

The defeat darkened her eyes. "I know. But maybe we should take two of these chairs and try to break one of the glass entrance doors…anything to get help here. If we can trip the alarm, we might not survive, but…"

She didn't have to say the rest. She couldn't bear to sit here and let those men destroy the Colby Agency without attempting to fight back.

Brad thought about that for a time. She was right. To sit here and let this thing go down without fighting back, armed or not, was just wrong.

He considered the exits and the complications they could encounter. Breaking that wall of glass at the front of the lobby would take a damned car being driven through it. He was reasonably certain a lightweight chair wouldn't get the job done. He doubted anything other than getting caught would be accomplished. And even then he couldn't be one hundred percent certain the alarm system would still work properly.

His thoughts kept going back to the maintenance area where he'd been beaten and bound. There had been a lot of small storerooms. And that one door that appeared to be an exit to the outside. He couldn't be certain without going back to check it out.

All he had to do was talk Elaine into staying put while he went back.

"Gibson."

He turned his head toward her. "Yeah?"

"Circumstances notwithstanding, I'm glad we met."

He wondered, if they survived this night would she want to visit him in prison. Because that was sure where he would end up if he didn't make it out of here with that evidence.

But they hadn't survived the night just yet. This moment was all they had.

If this was going to be his last night on earth, there was one thing he absolutely had to do before he died.

Chapter Twelve

3:02 a.m.

He kissed her.

Elaine hadn't expected it...but she'd found herself wishing.

And then he'd looked at her mouth and she'd taken that hopeful lean...

His lips felt softer than she'd expected. His touch was light, sensitive to her uncertainty. But a sweet sensation of yearning drew her closer, deeper into the kiss, and all that uncertainty vanished as if it had never existed at all. She placed her hand against his shirtfront, not to push him away but to feel the strong beat of his heart, to know that he was alive and that this moment incited the same rush of anticipation in his chest that it caused in hers.

No matter what happened as this night grayed into dawn, this moment was theirs.

They drew back at the same moment, both needing to catch their breath. His taste, even the tang of blood from his busted lip, made her hunger for more of him.

"I'm *very* glad we met," he murmured, his lips still near enough to kiss.

She resisted the impulse. As much as she wanted to feel his mouth on hers once more, they couldn't risk any more distraction.

"I don't know why they haven't killed us yet." She'd been thinking about this since she'd escaped. Something was really wrong with this whole picture. "But I don't want to hang around and find out. This feels wrong, beyond the obvious."

He nodded, his gaze settling comfortably onto hers. "They've been here all night. Getting what they came here for shouldn't have taken this long." He glanced back out toward the lobby. "These guys are professionals. Whatever they're up to isn't nearly so straightforward as they would have us believe. Not that I'm complaining." He grimaced. "At least we're still alive."

"You okay?" Both eyes were swollen, the damaged areas already darkening. His lip was split, not badly, just a little in one corner. At his skeptical look she answered her own question. "Yeah, I know. Dumb question." She remembered him asking her a similar question after she'd cut her leg. Wow. She hadn't even had time to think about her injury, but now that she did it stung viciously.

"Whatever is going down around here, it's not what it seems."

"I was thinking the same thing. This is off somehow. Pros would have been in and out quickly, and they sure wouldn't have wasted time running the two of us down again when they could have killed us in that files room more than an hour ago."

That was the part that nagged at Elaine the most. Why would a killer tell her she would survive? That it was his Christmas gift to her? It didn't make sense. Nothing about this entire night made sense.

She thought of those musicians somewhere out there in the cold, dead or dying. Most likely dead. If they had families, wives or husbands, children, brothers, sisters, parents…she blocked the endless possibilities. This would be the worst Christmas ever for those families.

Elaine felt sick to her stomach with regret. She should have called her mom and dad. It would have been so easy to call and say she'd be home early on Christmas Eve. She had the whole day off.

She hadn't helped Mildred put up the Christmas decorations, opting instead to take them down after New Year's. She'd behaved like a Scrooge, that was what she'd done. She hadn't cared about Christmas and she'd resented anyone around her who did. For no good reason.

Joseph and the other guard, those musicians, none of them would get to enjoy the life she had so frequently taken for granted in the past.

She promised herself then and there that if she survived this night she would be different from this point forward. She would join in, rather than stand back and watch. She would live life rather than let it pass her by.

Funny, how it took coming so close to death to realize just how precious life really was.

"I say we try to get out of here."

She held his gaze, the steadiness there inspiring complete confidence in his suggestion. It didn't seem possible that they could have known each other only a few hours. She felt as if she knew him better than anyone, maybe because they were both so battered and bruised. He'd lied to protect her, telling those men that he worked for the Colby Agency to protect her. She'd read about heroes and watched those guys who saved the day in her favorite movies. But she'd never had anyone come to her rescue like that. He had offered to trade his life for hers.

"I say you're right." She peered between the chairs to see if anything moved in the lobby as far as she could see. "If we don't get out of here now, there may not be another opportunity."

He got up first, groaning with the effort. He offered his hand and assisted her to her feet. As if by second nature, she surveyed the marble-floored distance in front of them. They had to make that journey back across the lobby, leaving themselves wide open to the enemy.

It was the only way.

They had to get out of this building.

It was a major risk, but one they had to take.

He took her hand and moved forward, careful to keep her one step back and slightly behind him. It felt dreamlike walking toward the main lobby the same way she did every morning and every night coming and going from work. Their clothes were dirty and damaged, bloody even. Their bodies were riddled with injuries, some minor others not so. She felt as if she'd been to war and she'd never even left the office.

At the corner where the corridor opened out into the lobby proper, he hesitated and listened. She did the same. The whole building seemed eerily quiet. The idea made her shiver. What the hell was going on here? Who were these people?

She blocked the questions. She should just be glad they weren't out here shooting at them.

Then again, no one had actually shot at them.

That realization gave her pause. The marble was icy under her bare feet. Why didn't they just shoot them when they had the chance?

Brad urged her to get moving again with a tug on her hand.

He was right. They needed to get out of the open. The longer it took to reach the other side of the lobby, the longer they were sitting ducks.

Reaching the corridor on the other side of the lobby that led to the stairwell provided some margin of relief. Without the soaring ceiling and towering wall of glass she felt somehow more concealed.

He didn't stop until he reached the stairwell door. She did the unlocking and they entered the stairwell, conscious of any sound. She wanted to ask where they were headed but didn't want to chance making the slightest noise.

That he chose the door that would take them down to the basement level rather than up to the next floor confused her, but she felt certain he had a plan or that going this route somehow facilitated his plan. He'd mentioned a door he thought led to the outside.

The corridor on the lowest floor of the building was narrower than the ones on the upper levels. The lighting, or lack thereof, only added to her uneasiness. But she'd been down to the mail room before on several occasions prior to this night's events so she wasn't entirely out of her element. It was only the maintenance section she'd never had the pleasure of visiting before.

When he made the turn that would take them in that direction she had to ask, "Did you say there's a way out where we're headed?" She hoped maybe there was another part of this level she hadn't seen. What little she'd glimpsed of maintenance when she'd found Gibson earlier hadn't looked promising. Still, he'd mentioned a door.

"There's a potential exit."

That he didn't slow down or look at her when he made the statement concerned her to some degree.

"Potential?"

"The sign above the door says exit, but it's locked so I'm not sure. It's worth a try."

He was right. It was worth a try.

Once Gibson felt confident he opened the door to maintenance.

"It worries me that this door is the only interior entry door that hasn't been locked," she felt compelled to say. When she'd come in here looking for him earlier she'd been too frantic to find him to care what obstacles lay on the other side of the door or to speculate why it wasn't locked. But now she wondered.

Following Gibson deep into the bowels of maintenance, she got that same feeling she did when she took her car in for routine inspection. The smell, she decided. Industrial and machinelike. The pipes and ductwork meandering overhead made her think of an ongoing construction site.

"Over here."

The exit sign was there all right. But an exit to where she couldn't say. There could be steps outside the door that led up to ground level. It did make sense, she decided, that this level would have an emergency exit the same as any other floor.

She tried the knob.

"It's locked," he said at the same time.

"I could try my keys." She was pretty sure that nothing on her ring would fit this door but she was willing to try.

"It wouldn't hurt." He looked around the room. "I'll look for something to use as a lever."

Anticipation at the idea that they could be out of here soon jostled her nerves.

But if this move did activate an alarm she just prayed they could get out the door and reach help before they were caught.

The tomblike quality the building had taken on since their escape had dread hardening in her belly. Where were the intruders? Were they still searching? Carrying off more Colby Agency files, electronic and/or paper?

She couldn't shake the feeling that the worst was yet to come. She wiggled the ring of keys out of her sleeve and tried every single one. No luck.

"We need tools," Gibson said then.

She followed his gaze as he surveyed the area, then locked in on several large, vertical tool boxes. Again she was reminded of a mechanic's shop.

Elaine wasn't sure what they were looking for but

she jumped in there and tried to help. He'd mentioned a crowbar. She knew what one of those looked like.

The tool box yielded nothing useful. Lots of small wrenches and a variety of screwdrivers. She picked up the stoutest-looking flat tip and measured its weight in her hand. This could help with prying near the lock.

"Can you use this?" She held up the hefty tool for Gibson to have a look.

"Maybe." He came away from his search with a heavy duty crowbar and a considerable-looking sledgehammer. "Between the two of us, I think we can take the door."

She smiled. He was right. They could do this.

That door didn't have a chance.

He hesitated. "How about I work on this door while you keep watch at the other? If we're both focused on escape, they might be on top of us before we even notice."

He was right. She should have thought of that.

"I'll get into place."

The need to say more was there but the time wasn't, so she hurried back to the door where they'd entered from the corridor and took up watch.

The corridor remained deserted and that whole impression of emptiness still resonated in the very air around her. Thick, almost suffocating in its intensity.

Weird.

If the bad guys had finished their work and left,

why had they allowed them to survive? Granted they hadn't seen their faces, but they'd heard their voices and could describe overall build. Even she, a mere receptionist, recognized those details weren't enough to nail these guys.

The groan of metal pierced the air.

Her gaze swung in Gibson's direction. She couldn't see what he was doing from where she stood but she could definitely hear him. She peered down that endless, nearly dark corridor beyond her point of watch. Still empty.

She prayed this plan would work.

Loud clanging reverberated across the distance between them, making her heart thump hard against her sternum. Anyone who didn't hear that was deaf.

She hoped he hurried.

Afraid to look away even for an instant, she kept her eyes glued to the corridor. She listened as best she could between bangs and groans coming from Gibson's work.

Two more slams of what was no doubt the sledge-hammer and silence reigned for several moments.

She'd started to get uneasy in the ensuing quiet when Gibson joined her at the door.

"Let's go."

The victory in his eyes sent a trill of excitement through her. Was this it? Were they finally going to put an end to this nightmare?

Gibson grabbed her hand and suddenly they were running toward the exit door he'd beaten free of its frame.

They were finally getting out of here.

The cold air hit her in the face like a pail of ice being thrown straight at her.

Her feet landed on the concrete outside the dented door and her breath evacuated her lungs.

Her knees buckled, which caused her to alternately stumble and lunge up the snow-covered stairs behind Gibson. She didn't slow down. Just kept going, pretending that her toes and feet weren't going numb.

She slipped twice, but Gibson pulled her back to her feet and kept pushing forward.

No looking back.

They topped the steps and the night sky, sans stars and with nothing more than a sliver of moon, greeted her.

Her chest constricted.

They were out.

They were free.

She did let herself look back now. No one appeared to have followed.

Or maybe they were already long gone.

The snow was ankle deep.

Her feet had gone completely numb, but she just kept going. Gibson ran, pulling her behind him, up the long alley between their building and its twelve-story neighbor.

She fell. She tried to get back up, except her feet just wouldn't cooperate.

"Dammit. I forgot about that."

Still struggling to get back on her feet, she was suddenly in his arms. He'd scooped her right up out of the icy blanket of snow.

"Why didn't you say something?"

As good as it felt to be in his arms, she couldn't help glancing back down the alley. This was no time to be worried about a little frostbite. "We have to keep moving, Gibson."

Her words prodding him back into action, he raced for the front of the alley. The temptation to rest her head against his shoulder was nearly irresistible. But she had to stay alert. Watch for trouble.

What they needed was a phone, but a passing car would work just fine. Anything.

If an alarm had sounded it was a silent one linked directly to the police.

She prayed there would be traffic out at this hour. Someone who could drive them to the closest precinct.

Her legs were freezing, so was her face. The snow had stopped falling but the wind was sharp and biting.

Gibson ducked around the corner of the building next door and backed into an alcove of sorts created by a trio of columns nestled close to the front wall.

Her body had started to shake involuntarily from the cold. She tried to control it, but that wasn't happening. Why had she worn those boots today? Her mother had always advised her that wearing high heels was bad for the feet. Bad for the legs even, she would say. Never once had she warned that they could get you killed.

"I can stand," she offered as her senses absorbed the price Gibson paid for supporting her weight, much less having run nearly a block while carrying her. Those men had beaten him pretty badly. He could have injuries not readily visible. Lugging her around could be causing additional damage. "Really, I'm okay now."

He glanced down at her naked legs and feet. "You'll freeze to death. Let's just take a moment to think."

She wasn't the only one who was cold. As warm and strong as his arms felt beneath her, she could feel the slight tremor in his body. Holding her like this while fighting off the brutal cold couldn't be easy.

The moments that ticked by, heavy with silence, drew her gaze to the street he'd been surveying since the moment they ducked behind cover.

Discounting the Christmas lights and streetlights, the whole block, in either direction, looked dark and deserted. The silence was the worst part. Even the sound of her jagged breath seemed to echo on and on in the stillness.

They were alone.

Completely alone.

Not even the bad guys had come after them.

"Do you think they left?"

The entire scene felt surreal.

Killers dressed entirely in black had chased and tortured them for the past seven or eight hours. Now they had finally escaped and it was as if they were the only two people in the world.

The streets were empty.

The world had gone to bed and was sleeping soundly in anticipation of the arrival of Christmas Eve.

"I don't know, but it sure looks that way."

Elaine squeezed her eyes shut then opened them wide. "If it weren't so damned cold out here I'd swear we were both dreaming."

A somber mask fell over his face. "I have to go back."

Shock rumbled deep inside her. He couldn't have said what it sounded like he said. "You're kidding, right?"

He shook his head, his gaze dead serious. "I need that pouch."

The evidence. He needed it to clear his name. She bit her bottom lip and considered any possible alternatives. "You don't trust that it'll be okay until we can get the police over here?"

"I don't know. Something about this whole thing feels wrong. I'm not sure I should take the risk."

She wiggled to get loose, forcing him to let her down. "Fine. We'll go back in together." He wasn't the only one whose instincts were protesting.

"No. You need to head over a street or two and look for help." He lifted his right foot and slipped off his shoe, then did the same with the left. "Wear these. They'll be way too big, but at least they'll give you some protection against the cold."

Men! "I'm not taking your shoes. Then your feet will freeze."

He thrust the shoes at her. "But I'm going back inside where there's no snow and the temperature is at least fifty degrees."

He had her there, but it didn't make her like it any better.

"Just run as fast as you can for help. There's a bar and grill on the Mag Mile about four blocks from here. Mack's."

She nodded. "I know that place."

"The owner lives on the second floor. Make enough noise and he'll hear you."

Mack's. She knew exactly where the place was. She could make lots of noise. "But what if—"

"They're probably gone already." He ushered her toward the sidewalk. "Go, Elaine, get help."

And then he was gone.

She'd wanted to say something more just in case… but it was too late now. She edged to the corner of the building, watching him disappear down the steps that led to the basement-level entrance.

He was probably right. Those guys were likely long gone.

She hugged her arms around herself. Okay. All she had to do was get help on the way.

No problem.

She plodded through the snow, her toes curled to keep the shoes from popping off. Four blocks. Over one block and then left for three blocks. She knew the way.

Ignore the cold. Her body shuddered in spite of her order, but she just kept going.

She thought about steaming hot chocolate and warm bowls of fried rice, two of her favorite foods. That would be her first order of business when this was over. Food. She was starved.

And she was freezing.

She shivered.

Keep going.

Don't think about it.

She stopped in the middle of the street. She'd pretty much been moving up the middle since she started running.

Headlights turned onto her street.

An SUV.

Thank God.

She waved her arms. "Hey!"

The vehicle kept coming.

"Hey!" She moved away from the middle of the street, kept up the frenzied waving. "Help! Please. I need help!"

The SUV rolled to a stop next to her and the relief made her wobble precariously.

"Thank God."

She moved up to the door in anticipation of the window being lowered. She opened her mouth to thank the driver for stopping, but the words died in her throat.

"Get into the car, Miss Younger."

The man wearing the mask looked exactly like all the others she'd encountered this night, but the voice was undeniably familiar.

It was him.

The one who'd promised her survival as a Christmas present.

The weapon pointed at her face was a pretty good indicator that he'd changed his mind.

"Get in," he repeated, "or you'll die where you stand."

If he were here, alone, did that mean the other two were still in the building…with Gibson?

Chapter Thirteen

3:49 a.m.

Brad didn't encounter any problems slipping back into the building through the maintenance entrance. He used extreme caution as he moved through the room, working his way around dozens of places too easily used for concealing the enemy. He felt as if he'd fallen into a video game where he'd been programmed to lose.

At the door to the corridor he took his time and listened until he'd satisfied the instincts humming fiercely inside him.

Something was wrong with this whole picture. Off-kilter somehow.

When he would have moved into the corridor that would take him to the mail room, a loud thud had his attention swinging back to the alleyway exit.

The door had slammed shut.

He crouched behind the nearest vertical toolbox and listened for any sound that would indicate the enemy had either followed him back inside or had been waiting for him to return. As much as the latter didn't measure up to strategic logic, it felt exactly like what had taken place.

A single pounding crash against that exit door had him bracing for fight or flight. More thuds and bangs. But the sounds came from outside as if someone were trying to beat his way back inside.

Thirty seconds or more passed with no movement, no sound. He moved then. Retraced his zigzagging path back to that exit—his exit to freedom. He waited by the door for a time, just to make sure someone wasn't lying in wait to make a move when he exited. No attempt was made to come inside. Not the first sound.

But someone had been out there. Someone had slammed the door shut and made plenty of noise in the process.

He couldn't keep wasting time. Elaine was out there alone, going for help. He didn't want to leave her on her own any longer than necessary.

He reached for the door, gave the knob a twist and pushed.

He met the same resistance one would hitting a brick wall. He tried again. The door didn't budge.

He used his shoulder and went against it with his full body weight.

The door bounced a little but nothing more.

Why the hell would they lock him inside the building?

And if they were out there…with Elaine…then she could be in trouble.

He rammed at the door over and over with no luck. Whatever had been jammed against it, it wasn't moving.

To hell with the pouch. He needed out. He needed to get back to Elaine. He should never have let her go anywhere without him. Big mistake. It was her they'd come here for. Her and those Colby Agency files.

What an idiot he was!

He'd selfishly thought this whole thing was about him and Welton. He'd been too obsessed with that possibility to see the facts right in front of him.

He had to find another way out. He grabbed the sledgehammer in case he needed it…closest thing to a weapon he had.

Running full throttle, he made it across the room to the corridor door before the thought had fully formed in his head. Just as he reached for the door something in the edge of his vision snagged his attention.

He turned around slowly, recognition filtering through the haze of denial even before he had the unexpected object in full view.

Bomb.

Brad was walking toward the object before his brain kicked into gear and told him to stop.

He stared at it, tucked neatly onto a wall shelf. A rectangular block of what looked like modeling clay, only with a gadget stuck into the middle of it that looked electrical.

Detonator.

The gadget was a detonator.

C-4.

He'd never personally seen the explosive but he instinctively understood this was what the material was. The detonator would likely be an explosive as well that would work as a propellant to activate the charge.

They intended to blow up the building.

He whirled toward the blocked exit.

He was trapped.

Eighth floor is prepped.

Help Bauer with six.

Was every floor rigged?

One or all, he was a dead man.

He turned back to the block of C-4.

Maybe he could somehow stop the reaction by preventing the first step in the process.

He knew almost nothing about explosives, except that they went bang and people died.

His pulse shifted into overdrive. Wait. He did know that an explosive like C-4 required a detonator. He'd seen enough news reports on terrorist acts to know that. The explosive he was looking at right that second definitely had what he would call a detonator. C-4 was basically harmless without a detonator.

Before he could talk himself out of it he walked over to the shelf, reached up and touched the detonator—or what he presumed to be the detonator.

Nothing happened. So he pulled it free from the C-4. He didn't throw it or drop it as his first impulse urged—he placed it carefully on top of the nearest tool box several feet away from the C-4.

When nothing blew up, he exhaled a lungful of pure terror.

Would this be the only one on this floor?

He turned all the way around.

In this area?

He made a quick sweep of the maintenance area and didn't see anything else. He hoped like hell he hadn't missed more of the stuff, but there wasn't time to be as thorough as he would like to be. He knew for certain the eighth floor was *prepped*.

Damn. If he only had Elaine's keys he could use the freight elevator. He'd have to settle for the stairs. But first he had to check the rest of this floor.

The corridor and restrooms were clear. He found another prepared charge in the mail room. It wasn't hidden or otherwise disguised. He carefully removed the detonator and laid it on a desk several feet from the C-4.

While he was in the mail room he grabbed the pouch, removed the jump drive and tucked it into his pocket. Might as well have it with him in the event he did somehow make it out of this sticky situation.

He took the stairs to the first floor two at a time. He didn't bother with any precautions. There was no one left in the building but him. That much he was certain of.

The first floor appeared to be clear. Nothing in the lobby, corridors or restrooms. The snack shop was still locked up tight. Newsstands were clean.

A thought occurred to him then—if whoever was in charge of this plan of destruction decided to detonate his handiwork, Brad would be screwed if the upper floors blew before he got to them. Common sense dictated that it would be better to start at the top and work his way down. Then again, if the place blew, he was dead either way.

He ran all the way up to the eighth floor without slowing, except once and that was to beat his way past the door at the second floor. He'd abandoned the sledgehammer after that. Two heavy, slowed him down.

As soon as he exited onto the eighth floor he realized something had changed.

The stairwell doors were no longer locked.

He tried the first office he came to…unlocked.

What the hell?

No time to analyze that right now.

He quickly checked each office, the restrooms, conference room and reception. Two charges, one on each end of the building.

Seventh floor.

Clean.

No charges he could find.

Had they opted to load only the even-numbered floors?

That would include Welton Investments as well as the Colby Agency.

Was that the rationale behind this entire scheme? It felt exactly as if there were no rationale to any of this.

Sixth floor, two charges, same location as the eighth.

Would his luck hold out to make it to the rest of the floors?

Not if he stood around asking rhetorical questions.

Fifth was clean.

Four…the Colby Agency.

He checked the west and east ends of the building first, found the charges in the same locations as floors six and eight.

Reaching for the stairwell door, he hesitated. If this floor was the target, would there be additional charges somewhere in the offices or the lounge?

He'd have to come back to this floor after he'd checked the final two. He had to work under the assumption that these bastards had a method, two charges per floor, even numbers, discounting the basement level.

Decision made, he descended to the third floor. Clean.

A cold sweat had broken out on his skin by the time he reached the second floor. He'd been too damned lucky so far. He'd removed all those detonators and nothing had happened.

What were the odds that his good fortune would hold out?

He entered the second floor and checked the areas where he'd found the charges on the other floors. Same scenario. He removed the detonators in each case, moving a little faster and with a lot more confidence.

He should go back to the fourth floor to check for more charges but his gut was telling him to spend a little more time on this floor as well.

"Why the hell not," he mumbled. The dead guy in the bathroom wouldn't care and Brad damn sure didn't want to join him.

He checked the restrooms, the lounge and the conference room. Clear.

Maybe his instincts were off on this one.

He moved from office to office and found every single door was unlocked. Incredible. How the hell had these guys manipulated the security system to meet their needs?

He located two more charges on the front side of

the building, located equal distances from the other charges. That puzzled him, and it also worried him that he'd missed similar charges on the other floors. As he checked the remainder of the offices, he defused—at least he hoped he did—two more charges on the back side of the building. That left only the more central portion of the floor untouched by the determination to bring the place down.

Strange.

The memory of those damaged elevator doors poked into his already jumbled thoughts. Just another part of this puzzle that didn't make a lot of sense. Not wanting to leave any stone unturned, he hustled back over to reception and checked the damaged shafts. Sure enough, there was a neat little package of C-4 in each one.

He made one final walk through in an effort to determine what it was that still nagged at him. He hesitated at his office, went inside and looked around one last time.

Then he saw it.

The housing on his CPU tower sat slightly askew. He walked to his desk and checked the housing. It pulled completely free of the tower. The interior of the tower had been tampered with…several parts, including the motherboard, were missing.

"Well, I'll be damned."

Chapter Fourteen

4:00 a.m.
Chicago's Mercy General Hospital

Victoria watched as her son ever so gently kissed his sleeping wife's forehead.

Tasha was exhausted, but it was a wondrous kind of exhaustion.

Little Jamie slept in a bassinet next to her mother's bed. She was absolutely beautiful. Just like her father, and her mother. Same midnight-black hair Jim had been born with that had lightened to a summer blond by the time he was six. It was too early to tell about the eyes yet. But Victoria was certain they would be blue just like the child's father and grandfather.

Lucas had gone for coffee. Victoria was fairly certain his decision to make the coffee run had more to do with his wanting to give her and her son some time alone than with the need for a beverage.

Victoria sensed that Jim wanted to talk. Lucas surely felt it as well. His instincts were even sharper than hers. She understood that the birth of this child had wielded a tremendous impact on Jim. She hadn't seen this kind of disquiet in him in almost a year. A part of her couldn't help being concerned. His well-being had been tenuous for so long. That he'd been well for most of this past year had allowed her to become complacent, to believe that the nightmares of his past were finally over.

Perhaps her conclusions were premature.

"Why don't we take a walk around the floor? We can peek in on the other babies in the nursery," she suggested when he joined her near the door.

He glanced back at his wife and child, then at the window. "The snow finally stopped."

Her instincts were right. He did want to talk. She worked at not jumping to conclusions, but it wasn't so easy.

Once they were in the corridor outside Tasha's room, they fell into a leisurely, matching stride.

They'd covered half the loop around the floor before he spoke. "I've been doing a lot of thinking the past few weeks."

"About your future?" This was the one area where her son still faltered. After being stolen from her at age seven, he'd spent nearly twenty years in pure hell. He'd suffered the worst injustices imaginable.

That he'd recovered to this extent was a miracle. No matter the great strides he'd made, he was still hesitant to dive into future career plans. Victoria would like nothing better than to have him at her side at the Colby Agency, the agency his father had started. But he'd resisted that step thus far.

"My future." He exhaled a burdened breath. "It's no longer just my future." He studied his mother for a moment before continuing. "Did you feel so determined to change the world when I was born?"

A smile spread across her lips. "Of course. Every mother and father does. It's part of the price we pay as parents."

He nodded and continued walking. "I know how much the agency means to you. How much it meant to my father."

There was a "but" coming.

"But I don't think it's the right place for me."

Victoria had suspected that this moment was coming. Though Tasha thoroughly enjoyed her part-time research work at the agency, Jim had no interest whatsoever. He didn't feel as if he fit in. He didn't have to say as much—Victoria had seen him with Ian and Simon and the others. Jim wasn't like them. He never would be. As much as it pained her to say that, she understood that was the case. The damage was far too great to expect him to go on with his life as if the past hadn't happened.

"Do you have something else in mind? A different kind of work we haven't talked about?" She wrapped her arm around his. "Your happiness is all that matters, Jim. You're free to make your own future. That has never been an issue. The Colby Agency was your father's dream, it became mine, but if it isn't yours, well that's okay, too."

Even as she said the words, some small amount of regret trickled through her. She had hoped Jim would come around. Evidently that wasn't going to happen.

Her son stopped and faced her. He looked so much like his father that she still lost her breath at times.

"The Colby Agency does a lot of good in this world, Victoria."

In the beginning, when he'd first come back to her, it had troubled her that he couldn't appear to get past calling her by her first name but she'd adapted. He loved her, he simply couldn't love her in the traditional manner, it wasn't in his makeup. Far too much humanity had been tortured out of him as a boy and then a young man. That he managed any emotion at all was a miracle really.

"But," he went on, "there are some wrongs that go beyond the reach of the police or private investigators or any other of the usual means of enforcing the rules and laws of society. Some wrongs can't be righted so easily."

The kind of wrong he'd suffered. She knew

exactly what he meant. He'd experienced the worst sort of horror. He was an expert in pain. He'd been baptized in the very flames of hell by the devil himself. A man can't experience that level of trauma without carrying the marks.

"I've decided," he continued, "that for those kinds of wrongs there has to be someone prepared to go beyond the law…to, at times, do what no one else will." He searched her eyes, tried to show her with his own what he could not with his expression or his voice. "I want to be that someone. I'll take the cases no one else will touch. I'll provide that equalizing element when all else fails. And no one or nothing will get in my way."

She understood completely. Her son wanted to fight the very evil that had stolen his life. He wanted to utilize for good the evil skills he had learned from the master himself. She could see that. In today's social climate there was a place for that equalizing element if used properly and only for good.

"When would you begin this new venture?" No point beating around the bush. If this was what her son wanted to do, then she would back him fully.

"In the New Year. I would like to be prepared to open up shop by mid January."

"Have you located office space yet?" She hoped he hadn't gotten that far with his plans without talking to her. Disappointment perched on the rim of her heart.

He shook his head. "I wanted your thoughts on that. Maybe we can pick out office space together. Tasha will have her hands full with the baby. This could be our project."

The disappointment faded and Victoria's heart lifted. "I know just the real estate agent to call. She can get started right away. I'm certain we'll have you in an appropriate office setting by New Year's. You'll need a minimal staff. Have you considered what you're looking for in the way of investigators just yet?"

A ghost of a smile haunted the corners of his mouth in that fleeting way that she'd come to recognize was the best her son could do.

"Not yet, but I think I'll know it when I see it."

Her arm still curled around his, Victoria resumed their journey around the floor. "What are Tasha's thoughts on the new venture?"

"She's a little worried, but she's trying hard to be supportive."

The business of which Jim spoke was one that frequently foraged into very dangerous territory. As a new mother, Tasha would certainly be concerned, but she loved her husband and Victoria knew she would do anything to see him happy.

If making a difference would do that, how could she or Tasha deny Jim that happiness?

"It sounds like you've thought this through very thoroughly, Jim. The cases are out there, there's no doubt. We can certainly refer cases of that nature to your firm, as I'm sure other agencies will do. It'll be just like in the beginning when your father and I started the Colby Agency, both thrilling and frustrating."

His gaze met hers. "I look forward to the challenge."

She could see that indeed he did. This was the venue for finding himself that her son had needed since making his way home. This was not sad news, this was a good thing. A step in the right direction.

"Ah, there's Lucas." She watched her husband step through the open doors as they approached the bank of elevators. "Let's share the good news with him."

As the two men in her life discussed these new plans for the future, Victoria experienced that old, haunting tug of uneasiness. She felt reasonably certain it wasn't about her son's decision. Not at all. This was that same disquiet she'd felt earlier tonight when she'd been decorating her Christmas tree.

Something was about to happen.

Every instinct warned that it was not good.

Chapter Fifteen

They were going to blow up the building.

Gibson was trapped inside.

Two men, including the one who appeared to be in charge, were holding her at gunpoint in the SUV.

The third man was out there somewhere checking out some last situation before the big bang. She grimaced at the pictures their words evoked. That was the way the guy in charge had put it.

She hated him already.

The radio crackled. Then a voice, the third man. She knew all their voices now. "We're a go."

The air turned to ice in her lungs. She couldn't sit here and let them do this. Gibson was in there!

She had to think fast.

"There's another file I'll bet you didn't know

about," she blurted. *God, please let this work. Please, please don't let them do this.* "That's where all the most important case details are stored."

The man turned from this position behind the wheel to look at her. She squirmed at the intensity in those hateful eyes. "Too late."

He pressed a button on the remote he'd been waving at her since forcing her into the SUV.

Her gaze swung to the building. Terror gripped her heart.

Nothing happened.

A lone snowflake or two drifted down outside the tinted window closest to her. The silence was so thick inside the vehicle she could barely take a breath. But the building was still standing.

Nothing had happened.

"What the hell?"

The man in charge wrenched his door open and stormed away from the SUV. He growled orders into the radio as he went, but Elaine only caught bits and pieces of what he said.

Whatever had gone wrong, they had only minutes to correct the problem. Time was short now. She didn't know why, but she understood that desperation had just kicked in.

The man in the front passenger seat watched, as did she, while his boss strode off into the alley between the two buildings, presumably to join his partner in crime.

Her fingers itched to grab the door handle and launch herself out of here. Would this man kill her if she made a run for it?

The one in charge had told her she was going to survive, that it was his gift to her. But then he'd pointed his weapon at her to force her into the SUV. So maybe he'd changed his mind.

She couldn't imagine why they cared whether or not she lived or died, but she got the definite impression that they did. Her instincts also warned her that these men considered Gibson expendable. Mounting anxiety twisted her in her belly. She had to do something.

The sound of the radio belonging to the man in the front seat had her hopeful for a distraction. If he were busy talking to the boss, she might be able to make a run for it. His delayed reaction might just give her time to get a head start.

She had to warn Gibson.

Her throat tightened at the idea that the building could blow at any moment and he was still inside.

"Don't let the girl out of your sight."

Elaine snapped to attention at the order barked over the airwaves. The man in charge's voice.

"She's right where you left her."

The man glanced back at her as if to verify his words. She looked away.

"Go ahead and get her into position."

Tension whipped through Elaine. What the hell

did that mean? Again she resisted the impulse to simply take her chances and run for it.

"Ten-four."

He put the radio away and opened his door.

Her breath caught as he then opened the back door. "Let's go," he ordered.

She clenched her toes inside Gibson's loafers. "Where're we going?"

"Shut up and get out."

She flinched. "Fine."

Was he taking her back into the building now? She wanted to be with Gibson. Wanted to help but what could she do to save him? Maybe not much.

She slid across and out of the seat, her borrowed shoes buried into the snow that proceeded to fill the empty spaces in the loafers around her feet. She shivered.

"This way."

He shoved her toward the parking area that flanked one side and the back of the building the Colby Agency called home. There were only three cars in the lot. Hers, another she figured was Brad's and then the colorful van she had the awful feeling belonged to the musicians.

The van appeared to be their destination.

He opened the rear cargo doors. "Get in."

She peered inside, couldn't see anything. The interior lights of the vehicle didn't come on.

"I said, get in!"

She climbed into the dark van. The instant she moved beyond the yawning doors and into the cargo area even without the ability to see, she encountered what she recognized on a very basic level was a dead body. A shriek popped out of her mouth before she could stop it.

"Lay down."

She shuddered, tried to reason with herself. She had to stay calm right now. She had to stay really calm. Whatever happened in the next few seconds or minutes could mean the difference between life and death for both her and Gibson.

Gathering her courage, she did as she was told. She tried not to think about the bodies, and there were more than one, piled into the vehicle with her. It was so cold in here. The skin she had touched when she first climbed into the van was as cold as ice.

The cargo doors slammed, closing her in with the dead.

Gibson. She had to focus on him. She couldn't let the fear get control.

Giving to the count of ten, she scrambled up to a sitting position, and angled herself toward the front window where she could watch the building.

She prayed that any second Gibson would come running out. But he didn't.

She had to do the running. Straight into that building to rescue him.

She watched as the two men, the one in charge and the third one she hadn't seen in a while, trudged through the snow on their way back to the SUV. The man who'd dragged her over here had already loaded back into the vehicle.

As soon as the final two had loaded up, she made her move. She tried to open the cargo doors. No luck. She couldn't unlock them.

She scrambled up to the front seat and tried both doors. Locked. The levers inside the vehicle should unlock the doors but they didn't. It was as if they, too, were under some kind of remote control like the security in the building where she'd worked. These men had planned this night to the last detail.

Fury slashed through her. They thought they'd won.

Well, she would show them. She'd watched a few search-and-rescue dramas in her time.

She leaned back onto the driver's seat and, using both feet, kicked at the passenger-side window as hard as she could. It took four tries, but the glass eventually fell away.

Her shoulder was too sore to do any wild diving, so she climbed out of the van a little more cautiously than she probably would have otherwise. She lost one of the loafers climbing out so she kicked the other one off. The snow was cold against her bare feet but she'd be able to run a lot faster without the shoes anyway.

She knew only one way she could get back into the building. The alley entrance that led into the basement was her only hope.

She heard a vehicle door slam and she ran as hard as she could. She didn't look back. Probably one of the men giving chase. If she looked back she might fall. Falling would get her caught. She had to make it.

She was almost to the corner of the building where the alley ran between it and the neighboring building when she heard him behind her. She could do it. Her feet had turned numb. Her legs shook, but she wouldn't slow. Wouldn't let him catch her. With a final burst of energy she plunged forward even faster.

Grabbing the handrail, she swung around to the descending steps and flew down them, almost falling twice. She'd reached the door and was pulling at the braces levered against it to keep anyone from coming out that way, when the man who'd given chase reached the top of the stairs.

She stared up at him.

For two beats she was sure he would be on top of her before she could get the door open. Adrenaline promoted her efforts and the heaviest brace gave way.

A blast of thunder discharged in the air. Vibration shook the earth.

No.

Not a vibration. Not thunder.

An explosion.

Fear rocketed through her.

Her gaze collided with that of the man who still stood at the top of the stairs. He suddenly moved but not toward her. He raced back in the direction they'd come.

The big bang had taken place and now they would leave. The masked men were finished with their dirty work. They wouldn't want to be caught by the police, who would no doubt come, alarm or no alarm.

The urge to cry rushed up from the depths of her soul.

Gibson.

Fury roared through right behind the softer emotion. She didn't have time to cry. Dammit. She had to find him.

Pushing aside the barriers strewn on the ground at her feet, she wrenched the door open and rushed inside.

"Gibson!"

The maintenance area appeared intact.

She ran across the room and into the lower-level corridor, then barreled onward toward the stairwell, where she encountered no obstacles. Since she didn't know where he was or where the explosion had hit, she had to check every floor to be sure. He could be anywhere.

The lobby was deserted. No telltale sign of the explosion. No Gibson.

Second floor maybe.

She took the stairs two at a time. Her leg had started to throb again and her feet were burning as if they'd caught fire, but she didn't care.

She called his name over and over, moved around the corridor on two and then headed up to three.

So far no destruction. What the hell had blown up?

She didn't find him on three.

Without slowing she raced into the stairwell once more. She'd just hit the landing between the third floor and the fourth and started that final flight of steps when she came face-to-face with the results of the explosion she'd heard and felt.

Parts of walls and slabs of twisted steel had spilled through an opening far larger than the original door had been. Bits and pieces of lush jewel colors were strewn amid the other debris.

Victoria's office.

They'd blown up the Colby Agency.

Her stomach dropped to her feet.

Had Gibson been on that floor?

She started forward with the intent of trying to dig through the debris but logic held her back. That wouldn't work, she'd only end up getting herself trapped.

There was only one way to access that floor.

Running as fast as her tingling feet would carry her she selected the restroom on the opposite end of the third floor, away from the damage on the fourth. She went into the final stall and got into position above the toilet, using the method Gibson had taught her. She slid the ceiling tile aside and grabbed onto the beam as if she'd been doing it her whole life. Her shoulder protested, the pain shooting along her arm and up her neck, but she ignored it, forcing her fatigued arms to pull her upward.

She moved along the beams until she reached the elevator shafts. It would have been nice to use the freight elevator but somewhere in the van with the dead musicians she'd lost her keys, and God only knew if the elevator even still worked at this point. Thankfully the emergency lights continued to operate.

She stared up the ladder and swallowed back her fear. She'd climbed it before. She could do it again.

But she'd had Gibson with her then.

Bracing one foot on the lowest rung, she reached up and grabbed on. She didn't let herself think about the devastation she'd seen that had once been Victoria's office. If she dwelled on that reality she wouldn't be able to focus on this one. Gibson could be up there, he could need her help. She had to focus.

As she moved upward, she thought of all the supplies she'd ordered. Reams of printer paper, file folders, pens—God, tons of pens. Her job was important. She kept the investigators in supplies. They needed her. Courage slipped into the mix of fear and anxiety. The Colby Agency needed her and Gibson needed her.

Her parents needed her, too.

They would miss her if anything happened. Maybe they weren't as demonstrative as other parents, but that didn't mean they didn't love her. Her mom called her every night. Her parents had always been there for her when she needed them. And from this day forward, Christmas and birthdays and every damned holiday of the year was going to be significant. They were going to celebrate as if it were their last day on earth.

She had a social life to develop and she damned well wanted to start with Brad Gibson.

He'd kissed her socks off. Well, okay, she hadn't been wearing socks, but he'd made her toes curl. She wanted more than that one kiss from him. She wanted more from life, period. It was no one's fault but her own that she'd let her life become a humdrum of nothingness other than work.

That evil bastard in the black mask had done her a huge favor—he'd let her survive this for whatever reasons as his so called Christmas gift. The way she saw it this second chance had come from a much higher source than that jerk and she damned well wasn't going to let it go to waste.

She reached the ceiling area above the fourth floor and stepped off the ladder.

After surveying the area above the Colby Agency it was clear the whole of the devastation was on Victoria's end of the building. The other side appeared normal.

Her nose wiggled in distaste. What was that smell?

Realization tore through her brain, sending fear racing along her limbs.

Gas. The kind used for heating the building.

She had to move.

As quickly as she dared she reached the area over the restroom and went through the steps to lower herself down. This time she did so over the counter area. She should have thought of that before. The counter that held the sinks sat up substantially higher than the toilets. Man, that would have been so much easier for her.

She'd have to remember that in the future.

Not that she planned on climbing around like this again anytime soon, but one never knew. After all, she worked for the Colby Agency. Even the receptionist needed combat training, it seemed.

The smell of gas had started to make her nostrils raw. She had to find Gibson and get him out of here.

As much as she wanted to lunge down the corridor, she took it slow. She couldn't be sure of the damage or debris she might find, so she took her time. On this floor the emergency lights blinked occasionally as if the electrical connection had been damaged in some way.

Between that and the smell of gas her nerves were wrecked. "Gibson!" She shouted his name over and over with nothing but her own echo for a response.

Where the hell was he?

She checked each office she passed. Everything beyond the lounge was pretty much a mess. What used to be Mildred's office was now a billowing hole beyond which Elaine could see the snow-covered parking area that spread out beyond that side of the building.

At least the hole allowed fresh air to come in and dilute the gaseous smell. Let in the cold, too. She shivered.

But did that mean it was safe? Just because the smell of gas wasn't so strong near this opening to the outside, was it less dangerous?

She didn't know for sure. Better safe than sorry. She had to find Gibson and get the hell out of here.

"Gibson!"

She'd just reached the debris line when something moved.

She whirled around, certain the sound had come from behind her. Shock kept her feet nailed to the floor and her mouth gaping.

The wall that separated the corridor from the conference room shifted right in front of her eyes.

"Holy cow."

Was more of this level going to fall apart?

She had to run.

She ran back the way she'd come. The wall crumbled right behind her, filling the corridor with crumbling drywall and strips of metal and wood, as well as insulation.

The lights dimmed, then brightened.

Damn.

She couldn't get beyond Victoria's office. That put the files room and other offices beyond her reach. The only thing she could think to do was go overhead again and try to move tiles over each area to see if he were trapped inside one of the remaining rooms.

Hesitating outside the ladies' room door, she decided she'd better check the men's room. It was about the only place on this end of the building she hadn't looked. It was empty. No Gibson.

Using the sink counter again, she climbed overhead once more. This time, however, the ladder wasn't her destination. She moved to the other side of the space above the fourth floor, and carefully started to remove ceiling tiles above each office she hadn't been able to access.

Nothing.

Until she reached the files room.

Part of the wall that separated the files room from the corridor beyond it had collapsed. Gibson lay on the floor near the edge of the destruction.

Panic sent her heart into an alarming rhythm.

She moved to a location over the filing cabinets and scrambled down. She slid off the file cabinets and rushed over to where Gibson lay on the floor.

There was blood.

Renewed terror poured through her veins.

Okay, not so bad, she told herself. Just a bump to the forehead. His skin felt warm.

Thank God.

She leaned down and put her face close to his. The feel of his breath on her cheek had her shuddering with relief.

Thank God. Thank God.

"Gibson." She shook him gently. "Wake up, we have to get out of here."

He moved.

Hope expanded in her chest.

"Gibson." She shook him again. "Come on, we have to get out of here."

He opened his eyes, blinked a couple of times.

"We have to hurry." She sniffed. "Smell that, it's gas." She didn't mention the fact that another wall had fallen since she'd gotten here. He might not even realize what had happened.

"Elaine?"

She nodded. "Let's go." She helped him to a sitting position. The gash on his forehead appeared to be his only injury. "You think you can stand up?"

"Yeah." He got up, looked a little shaky. "What the hell happened?" He stared at what had been the wall that separated the files room from the corridor.

"An explosion."

He looked at her, then seemed to remember something. "I thought I'd gotten them all. I came back here to check."

She didn't understand what he meant and there was no time for questions. "We have to hurry."

Using a chair, she climbed back onto the filing cabinets and up through the ceiling. Gibson followed the route she had taken, his movements clumsier than before. She hoped that didn't mean his injury was worse than she'd suspected. She couldn't allow herself to think of all the things that could be wrong. Maybe he was just shaken up.

She sure as hell was.

Keeping a close eye on him, she led the way back to the ladder. The smell of gas was stronger now, stifling. They had to hurry.

"Do you think you can do this?"

She'd been the one who fell off the ladder and now she was worried sick he wouldn't be able to go down one floor. That's all they had to do. Down one floor and then they could use the stairwell.

The idea that the intruders could remotely detonate something else had fear turning her stomach into knots of panic.

"I think so."

She decided it would be best if she went first. She didn't know if she could stop him from falling but she wanted to be in a position to try.

Moving more slowly than she would have liked, they made it down to the third level. All they had to do now was drop down into the restroom and head for the stairwell.

She reached the area where she wanted to exit, crouched down and slid a tile aside. She'd just started to lower her body through the opening when Gibson lost his balance. She tried to hang on with one hand while reaching for him with the other—it didn't work.

Crashing through the ceiling, the counter below broke her fall and sent pain shooting up her backside.

Gibson hit the counter, then the floor.

She moved too quickly and ended up on the floor herself.

"You okay?" He was the first one on his feet.

"Yeah, I think so." She took his hand and let him help her to her feet.

"Sorry about that. A wave of dizziness hit me and—" He shrugged.

This could mean he had a concussion. "Let's just get out of here."

The smell of gas was even stronger on this floor. They could hardly breathe.

Keeping a hold on his hand, she walked quickly

to the stairwell. She wanted to move faster but she worried whether he could handle it, so she used a bit more caution.

When they reached the basement level, she did break into a run. They had both started to cough.

The emergency lights kept dimming and then brightening. They could go out at any second and that would make getting out of the building a lot more difficult.

She cleared the door to maintenance and was halfway to that exit to the alley when things went black.

Stopping dead in her tracks, she blinked rapidly to adjust her vision. Then she started moving again. She held on tightly to Gibson's hand. They had to get out of here. There was no way to guess what would happen next.

Since the door still stood open the white of the snow that had blown in led her right to it.

They rushed up the stairs, slipping and sliding on the snow-covered steps. Every instinct railed at her to move faster. To get as far away from the building as possible. Sirens blared in the distance.

Help was finally on the way.

They burst out of the alley and rushed to the other side of the street, their feet slipping this way and that. If her feet were burning now she could no longer feel them.

Lungs heaving, she flattened against the building on the opposite side of the street. They'd made it.

Gibson leaned against the wall next to her. "Looks like we lived through the night after all."

"Yeah." She gulped down more air, couldn't seem to get enough into her lungs.

Fire trucks and police cruisers were roaring toward them now.

Thank God. It was finally over.

Elaine stared at the dark building that was home to the Colby Agency. They were both still alive. Lights flickered in the dark building. The emergency lights trying to come back on, she presumed.

The explosion took her by surprise.

It shook the sidewalk beneath her feet.

Debris showered down around them.

She was suddenly on the ground with Gibson on top of her, protecting her with his body.

Out of nowhere someone was hovering over them asking questions but she couldn't hear the words.

Gibson struggled to his feet, helped her up. The man talking to them—the man she couldn't hear—wore a uniform. Paramedic.

Red and blue lights pulsed, making her eyes hurt. Policemen and firemen were everywhere.

Her gaze moved beyond the flurry of activity to the building they'd exited mere minutes earlier.

Flames reached out of every shattered window. Smoke rose above it like the mushroom cloud from a nuclear blast.

Several seconds were required for her mind to assimilate what all that she saw meant.

Something, the gas maybe, inside the building had exploded. Not just one explosion, a series of explosions.

Two more paramedics had crowded around them, were ushering them to move to a safer location.

"We have to move now!" one shouted.

She heard him but the sound was lower than it should have been.

"Hurry, ma'am."

Gibson grabbed her hand and tugged her toward him. He apparently understood the orders better than she.

The whole procession suddenly stopped and her gaze swung back to the flaming building.

It started to collapse, one floor dropping down onto the other, folding into itself.

Elaine couldn't move.

She could only stare at the flames licking upward against the dark sky.

It was gone.

She couldn't believe it.

The Colby Agency was gone.

Chapter Sixteen

Christmas Eve 6:15 p.m.
The home of Lucas Victoria Colby-Camp

Brad felt slightly out of place in Victoria's home. But with the morning's events the Colby Agency party had been relocated here.

He'd met only a handful of the people present. Mildred, Victoria's assistant, who was accompanied by her husband, Dr. Austin Ballard. Ian Michaels and his wife Nicole. Simon Ruhl with his wife Jolie. Most of the others he had not met before. And he hadn't met any of the aforementioned wives.

And then there was Elaine.

At the hospital this morning her leg had been patched up by a professional, though the doctor had complimented Brad on his work. Not that he'd been there to hear the compliment, he'd been in the middle of a CT scan that was followed by X-rays. Mild concussion and one fractured rib. The gash on his forehead had been taped rather than stitched. He had various other bruises and was basically sore as hell. A long, hot bath had helped a little with the soreness.

Mainly, he was just glad to be here. The evidence had been turned over to the special agent in charge of the Bureau's case against Welton Investments and Brad knew he would be cleared. There would be a few hoops to jump through, statements and then the trial, but he wasn't worried. He was innocent and he had the evidence to prove it.

Elaine had torn a ligament in her shoulder. She had a couple dozen stitches in her thigh and, like him, was damned sore with too many bruises and scrapes to count. They'd both come close to having frostbitten toes.

Five innocent people had died. The three musicians and the two security guards. The three men in the SUV were still at large. There was a good chance they might never know who they were. But Brad knew who they weren't. Those men hadn't overtaken the building to get to the Colby Agency; last night's events had been about Welton. The files they had taken from the Colby Agency had been a ruse to make it look as if the destruction was ordered as an act of revenge by an enemy of Victoria's. Not the case at all.

Every single computer in Welton Investments had been tampered with. Rather than wiping the hard drives, they'd simply removed the elements that housed the memory and so forth, leaving the towers to look untouched. Had he not noticed the loose housing on his own computer. No one might ever have known. That's why there had been five times more charges set on the second floor than any other. The Colby Agency was merely a way to make it look as if the Welton files, that were about to be subpoenaed by a federal warrant, had been damaged beyond retrieval. That was the reason for the men ensuring that Elaine survived. She would tell how the men had forced her to give up her username and password. Both she and Brad had witnessed the CPUs and files being taken from the Colby Agency files room. No one would have been the wiser and the Bureau would have had no evidence against Welton and no way to prove they had purposely destroyed it.

The perfect plan.

Except Brad and Elaine had been far more worthy opponents than the men sent to do the damage had anticipated.

Speaking of Elaine, where had she gotten to?

He moved through the crowd until he discovered her near the fireplace chatting with Victoria. He could understand why she felt the need to stay near the fire. They'd both been half-frozen by the time an ambulance had transported them to Mercy General.

Victoria smiled at Brad as he neared. "Brad, we

were just saying how wise it was of you to ensure you got out of there with the evidence to take Welton down."

He nodded, considering the statement high praise from a woman like Victoria.

"In fact," she went on, "I was just telling Elaine that I felt certain you were going to be one of our very best investigators. Given her recounting of your bravery and your ability to use your wit and intelligence in the absence of weapons, I'm convinced we were lucky to get you."

"Thank you, Victoria." He turned to Elaine. "But we wouldn't have survived if it hadn't been for Elaine. She was amazing."

Victoria pointed a knowing look at her receptionist. "After the holidays we're going to talk about moving you into investigations as well, Elaine, unless you prefer to stay where you are."

Judging by the glow that lit in her eyes, Brad was pretty sure she was excited by the idea.

"I'd like that," she admitted.

"Well, I'd better mingle a little more."

Victoria moved into the crowd, leaving them alone by the fire. It was the first time since they'd arrived that they'd had a minute to themselves.

"Do you know all these people?" he asked, scanning the elegantly dressed crowd.

She directed his attention to an older, distinguished looking man. "That's Lucas Camp, Victoria's husband. Over there, talking to Victoria now, is Jim, her son. I'll have to tell you all about him later, it's complicated."

The man, Jim, looked complicated, Brad decided. There was an edginess about him. Something hard and determined.

"You know Ian and Simon."

He nodded, dragging his attention from Jim Colby. "But what about that group over there."

"Okay." She described attire as she went so he'd know who she'd just named without her having to point. "Ethan Delaney and his wife Jenn. Her father is Mildred's new husband. Ric Martinez and Piper Ryan. Piper is Lucas's niece. Oh." She leaned closer and directed his attention to the bar. "Now those guys, they're like these living legends. That's Jack Raine, his wife Katherine is around here somewhere. And next to him is Trevor Sloan, Rachel is his wife. She has the dark hair and exotic looks. Then we have Nick Foster and his wife Laura. Pierce Maxwell and his wife Scout. Ryan Braxton and his wife Melaney. Trent Tucker and his wife Kelly. Heath and Jayne Murphy."

She moved in close again. "Then we have Cole Danes and wife Angel. Angel is Mildred's niece. Alexandra Hayden and her husband Mitch. Doug Cooper-Smith and his wife Eddi. Amy Calhoun, she used to have my job, and her husband John. There's Todd Thompson and his wife Serena. Daniel and

Emily Marks. A.J. Braddock and his girlfriend Gabrielle Jordan. Keith and Ashley Devers. Oh, and Ben Haygood our resident computer guru and Patrick O'Brien—watch him, he's a shrink." She scanned the crowd once more. "Oh, I almost forgot Zach Ashton and his wife Beth. Zach's the agency's top legal eagle. I think that's it. Wow, it looks like *everyone* is here. No wait." She turned to the mantel over the fireplace. "I almost forgot." She pointed to a framed eight-by-ten. "This is Tasha, Jim's wife, and their new daughter Jamie."

Brad felt a little overwhelmed. "All these people work for the Colby Agency?"

"Most do. Some have moved out of the investigations business in order to have more time with their families. But they keep in touch. Joining the Colby Agency is like becoming part of a family." Her expression turned distant for a moment. "I didn't realize just how much so until recently."

Brad was just about to ask her if they could possibly find a moment's privacy when Victoria called for everyone's attention.

The whole room shifted their attention to the woman who had made the Colby Agency what it was.

"As you all know, the Colby Agency lost its home this day." Somber sounds of acknowledgement moved through the group. The faces of all present reflected the deep regret they felt for the tragedy. "Two fine men, Joseph Reynard and Howard Benningfield, lost their lives last night, as well as a trio of musicians who served our community bringing music to our homes and workplaces. It is a privilege to offer the families of those men whatever support, financial or otherwise, they may need in the coming months."

The crowd burst into applause.

When the applause had settled, Victoria went on. "Next I want to assure you that the Colby Agency will rise from the ashes. Better men than those who struck last night have tried to tear us down, to no avail."

Cheers went around the room.

"However, in reflecting on what we have accomplished at the Colby Agency in our twenty-plus years, I have decided that there are definite changes that need to be made. Some of you may know that my son, Jim, has decided to start his own firm in the New Year. I wish him the best of luck with his endeavor and have offered him my full support."

Another round of applause followed that announcement.

Elaine found herself holding her breath as Victoria continued.

"Many of you may have concerns as to what happens next with the Colby Agency. Rest assured that we are far from defeated. I have some very exciting new plans for our agency. All the details are not worked out as of yet, but I can tell you this, what we are about to launch is not only the very best of what we have had in the past, but a brand-new beginning that will go beyond all expectations. So—" she lifted her glass "—I offer a toast to the Colby Agency and its new beginning."

The excitement was contagious. More cheers and applause followed the toast. Elaine sipped her champagne, the bubbles tickling her nose. A new beginning. She was so thrilled to be a part of what would no doubt be a major turning point in Colby Agency history.

"I was wondering." Brad moved in close. "Do you suppose we could manage a moment alone? There's something I'd like to discuss with you."

"Sure." She set her glass on the nearest table. Brad placed his next to hers then followed as she led the way into a hall that wound around a corner, taking them far from the crowd in the main living area of the house.

She opened a door on the right and waited until he'd joined her inside before closing the door. "Is this okay? It's a guestroom."

He glanced around the room and immediately shifted his gaze away from the bed. "This is great."

Elaine's heart thudded so hard she could scarcely catch her breath. All evening she'd wanted to be alone with him, too, but there just hadn't been an opportunity. Now they were here and alone and she felt terrified. What if he didn't feel this all-consuming, overwhelming need to know her better, as she did for him?

"Last night was crazy and wild and pretty damned scary." He laughed, the sound tight and maybe a little nervous. "And I know that people bond during times of extreme stress and crisis and I also know that most of the time it doesn't last. But I think this thing that happened between us is more than that." He licked his lips, adding another layer of tension to her already soaring feelings of need and desire and plain old lust.

"Anyway, I'd really like to pursue this. I like you. I want to know you completely. I mean, if…if that's what you want to. If you're not—"

She silenced him with her mouth. It was enough already. She wanted to know him, inside and out. Every nuance. Every single thing. She wanted all of him.

The kiss went on and on. He held her in his arms and she hung on as tightly as she dared, considering he had a fractured rib. The kiss tugged at her senses making her want to dissolve right into his pores…to become a part of him.

When she had to catch her breath, she drew back, gasped for air. "We're going to have to leave this party early." She had just been offered a promotion; she wasn't about to get caught making love in her boss's guestroom.

"Any reason we can't leave right now?"

She shook her head. "Let's go. No one will notice."

He kissed her nose, then her lips, then her chin. "Your place or mine?"

She reveled in the feel of his strong body beneath her seeking hands. "I don't care. The car will be fine."

He smiled against her lips. "The car could work."

They stole out of the room, gathered their coats and slipped out the front door before anyone had noticed.

The snow had started to fall again, drifting slowly down as if there were no hurry since a good eight inches already lay on the ground. It was absolutely beautiful. The twinkling lights on the houses in the neighborhood took her breath away. She finally understood what all the hoopla was about.

It was about life and love and happiness.

It was about being grateful for every blessing no matter how small.

And it was about looking to the future with hope and zeal.

It was Christmas and for the first time in a very long time she understood what that meant. She'd called her folks and couldn't wait to spend the day with them tomorrow.

She slid into the passenger seat of Brad's car. He closed her door and moved around to get behind the wheel. She loved watching him move. The anticipation to be completely alone with him and in his arms was driving her crazy.

He started the engine and adjusted the heat to maximum. "Shall we go to my place? We could share something hot and sweet and finish decorating my tree. I never got around to finishing it."

She smiled. "That sounds perfect."

They buckled up and drove cautiously along the wintry streets of Chicago. It was as if she were seeing everything for the first time. She felt so alive and so on fire for the future.

Her gaze drifted back to the man who'd saved her life more than once and whose life she had saved a couple times as well.

Victoria was right, a new beginning was just what was needed.

A new beginning for her and Brad and a new beginning for the Colby Agency.

More exciting and more challenging.

That new beginning started right now.

* * * * *

Don't miss the new Colby trilogy
THE EQUALIZERS
featuring Jim Colby,
coming in April 2007.

New York Times *bestselling author*
Linda Lael Miller is back with a new romance
featuring the heartwarming McKettrick family
from Silhouette Special Edition.

SIERRA'S HOMECOMING
by Linda Lael Miller

On sale December 2006,
wherever books are sold.

Turn the page for a sneak preview!

Soft, smoky music poured into the room.

The next thing she knew, Sierra was in Travis's arms, close against that chest she'd admired earlier, and they were slow dancing.

Why didn't she pull away?

"Relax," he said. His breath was warm in her hair.

She giggled, more nervous than amused. What was the matter with her? She was attracted to Travis, had been from the first, and he was clearly attracted to her. They were both adults. Why not enjoy a little slow dancing in a ranch-house kitchen?

Because slow dancing led to other things. She took a step back and felt the counter flush against her lower back. Travis naturally came with her, since they were holding hands and he had one arm around her waist.

Simple physics.

Then he kissed her.

Physics again—this time, not so simple.

"Yikes," she said, when their mouths parted.

He grinned. "Nobody's ever said that after I kissed them."

She felt the heat and substance of his body pressed against hers. "It's going to happen, isn't it?" she heard herself whisper.

"Yep," Travis answered.

"But not tonight," Sierra said on a sigh.

"Probably not," Travis agreed.

"When, then?"

He chuckled, gave her a slow, nibbling kiss. "Tomorrow morning," he said. "After you drop Liam off at school."

"Isn't that...a little...soon?"

"Not soon enough," Travis answered, his voice husky. "Not nearly soon enough."

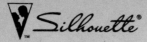

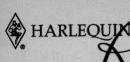

HARLEQUIN® Romance®

**From the Heart.
For the Heart.**

---

*Get swept away into the Outback
with two of Harlequin Romance's
top authors.*

Coming in December...

Claiming the Cattleman's Heart
BY BARBARA HANNAY

And in January don't miss...

Outback Man Seeks Wife
BY MARGARET WAY

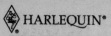

HARLEQUIN®

American ROMANCE®

IS PROUD TO PRESENT

COWBOY VET
by Pamela Britton

Jessie Monroe is the last person on earth
Rand Sheppard wants to rely on, but he needs
a veterinary technician—yesterday—and she's the
only one for hire. It turns out the woman who
destroyed his cousin's life isn't who Rand thought
she was. And now she's all he can think about!

"Pamela Britton writes the kind of
wonderfully romantic, sexy, witty romance
that readers dream of discovering
when they go into a bookstore."

—*New York Times* bestselling author
Jayne Ann Krentz

Cowboy Vet *is available from*
Harlequin American Romance in December 2006.

www.eHarlequin.com   HARPBDEC

REQUEST YOUR FREE BOOKS!

2 FREE NOVELS PLUS 2 FREE GIFTS!

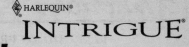

Breathtaking Romantic Suspense

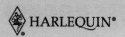

HARLEQUIN®

INTRIGUE®

COMING NEXT MONTH

#957 FORCE OF THE FALCON by Rita Herron
Eclipse
After a string of bizarre animal attacks near Falcon Ridge,
Brack Falcon finds a woman left for dead. But protecting
Sonya Silverstein means opening his long-dormant heart.

#958 TRIGGERED RESPONSE by Patricia Rosemoor
Security Breach
Brayden Sloane is a wanted man. He remembers an accident, an
explosion. Was he responsible? Only Claire Fanshaw knows for sure,
but how will she react to his touch?

#959 RELUCTANT WITNESS by Kathleen Long
Fate brings Kerri Nelson and Wade Sorenson back together to save
the life of her son, the only witness to a heinous crime.

#960 PULL OF THE MOON by Sylvie Kurtz
He's a Mystery
She's at Moongate Mansion for a story. He thinks she's an impostor.
But before history repeats Valerie Zea and Nicholas Galloway will
have to put their doubts aside to solve the mystery behind an
heiress's kidnapping.

#961 LAKOTA BABY by Elle James
Returning soldier Joe Lonewolf must enter the ugly underbelly of his
tribe if he's to rescue the baby boy he's never seen.

#962 UNDERCOVER SHEIK by Dana Marton
When Dr. Sadie Kauffman is kidnapped by desert bandits in Beharrain,
her only salvation lies in Sheik Nasir, the king's brother, who's trying
to stop a tyrant from plunging the country into civil war.

www.eHarlequin.com

HICNM1106